HUNT FOR GRACE

A WILLOW GRACE FBI THRILLER
BOOK 3

WITHOUT WARRANT

LIQUID MIND PUBLISHING

WILLOW GRACE SERIES

Willow Grace FBI Thrillers

Shadow of Grace

Condition of Grace

Hunt for Grace

Time for Grace

Piece of Grace (coming soon)

1 CHELSEA

Ever since I can remember, my dad has always told me, *Don't get dramatic, Chels.*

Not in a mean way, but in an, *in case things go sideways, stay calm*, sort of way. He started saying it when I was a little girl, when someone would take the swing I wanted on the playground or a teacher graded my science project extra harshly. My mom would always tell my dad that *he* was being a little harsh by telling me not to be dramatic, but I knew what he meant. He was telling me it was all going to be okay.

My dad and I were always two peas in a pod.

After my mom died when I was eleven and I felt like my whole world turned upside down – I remembered my dad's words. *Don't get dramatic, Chelsea.* Even though everything felt like it was turned on its head, I didn't have to be. I could stay calm. I could remember to take a deep breath.

I would repeat it over and over again when I fell asleep at night. *Don't get dramatic, Chelsea.* I would let myself cry for a few minutes, burying my head into the pillow, letting memories of Mom sweep me to sleep. But then I would wipe the tears from my eyes, exhale, and return to the present.

I'm thirteen now, and I'm not crying myself to sleep anymore, but I am repeating that mantra.

And in this moment, I am saying it more fervently than ever, which is saying something considering it was my saving grace after I lost Mom.

But Mom dying from cancer was more sad than scary.

Right now, I'm flat-out terrified.

"What are they gonna do to us?" a girl my age with dark brown hair, just like mine, asks softly. We don't want the men in the front seats to turn around and punish us.

Another girl answers, with tears in her eyes, "Probably kill us. Rape us first."

My eyes widen. *Don't get dramatic, Chelsea.*

There are five of us in the back of the van. I've never met any of the other girls before, never seen them. I was the third one captured. Our kidnappers drove around neighborhoods for hours as if just looking for girls the same age, the same size. It is hard to know if we were targeted or chosen at random. I'm guessing we're about the same age, but none of us has been very talkative – I think we are all too scared.

And the girl's words about being raped and killed, don't feel dramatic at all.

Because while I'm trying to be sensible, reasonable, a realist – which is what my father would've wanted -- deep down I know we are in trouble. Real trouble.

"Have any of you guys met before?" I finally ask. My voice is a whisper.

All five of us are sitting on the cold floor of the van. There are two men up front, one is the driver and the other is the man who dragged us into this vehicle. Our hands are tied behind our backs, our ankles bound together as well. Even if we could manage to open the back door, this van is barreling down the highway and there are cars surrounding us in four lanes of traffic. If we rolled out of the vehicle right now, we would be run over. It's not an option. The windows are all blacked out, but there is a strip of light on the bottom of the left side window.

"I've never seen any of you," one girl says softly. We all have long dark hair, but she has an air of innocence about her that I can see even in the darkness. Maybe it's the freckles across her nose. When I look at kids my age, I figure they are either the lucky ones, like her, or girls like me. Girls who have seen more heartbreak than a 13-year-old should.

Of course, now, we're all experiencing a new level of pain. Because whatever comes next, it's not gonna be good. Five girls, barely teenagers, all kidnapped after school. Headed to an unknown location by men who mean to do us harm.

The other girls are crying. Leaning on one another's shoulders, shaking. I must stay strong.

"We have to focus," I whisper. "We need to be smarter than these men."

It's dark now, the first week of November, the sun set hours ago. I have no idea where we are, and with the windows all blacked out, I can't make heads or tails of where we're being taken. And even though I don't know all the towns in greater Seattle, there are markers I could use. Ones my dad taught me to use. Mount Rainier in the distance, the Cascades or the Olympics. The Tacoma Narrows Bridge or the Puget Sound, or even the ferry system that has boats crisscrossing the water. If I could see any of those things, I would have some indication of where we might be. But right now, there's nothing to go on except the full moon hanging overhead.

"How are we supposed to be smarter than the men who kidnapped us?" asks another girl, still in her school soccer uniform. Practice must have just ended when she was taken.

"If they open the car door, we have to spring into action," I say. "We need to catch them off guard." I look around at the girls, wanting to see at least one of them holding on to hope. If everyone begins to fall apart, we will have no chance of surviving whatever comes next.

The freckle-faced girl nods. It surprises me because her eyes are chocolaty brown, and she looks so sweet, but when she speaks I feel foolish for assuming she wasn't as smart as me. "You're right. We can roll over and kick at them," she murmurs. "And we all need to do it at the same time, so we can freak them out; they won't see it coming. There's five of us and two of them."

"Right, and we can try again to get ourselves free," I say, adding on to her ideas. The other girls cry silently.

We spent hours when we first got in the van, trying to break the knots loose at our ankles and our hands, but we didn't get anywhere. It was hard to do without drawing the attention of the men. Still, it's better than sitting around, feeling like we're about to meet our maker. The redhead and I scoot closer to one another and begin fumbling with the knots on the ropes. Leaning in close to her, I ask her name.

"Ruby," she says. "You?"

"I'm Chelsea. Listen, the other girls are too scared to fight. So we have to stick together."

Ruby nods. The van hits a bump and swerves hard to the right. We roll away from one another, all of us sliding around on the floor.

"I think it's a flat," the driver says. The passenger looks over his shoulder at us as van pulls to a stop.

"Don't move," he hisses at us. Then looking at the driver he adds, "there's a spare in the back, tools too. Give me a sec."

My heart pounds. When we swerved, I rolled against something sharp. I reach for it and see that it's a screwdriver. I couldn't see it in the dim light of the van, but now it's literally rolled into the palm of my hand. "Ruby, come here." Her eyes widen, and she moves close. I jam the screwdriver through the knots at her wrists, loosening them.

They turn the van off, and both men exit the vehicle. I hand Ruby the screwdriver, and she loosens my knots. Then with our hands free,, we're able to quickly move to untying our feet. The other girls look at us, scared, but there's no time to help free them too. I have to act quickly. I give one of them the screwdriver as the passenger opens the back door of the van.

I see a tire iron wedged between the toolbox and the door. I lunge for it, taking hold of it before the man realizes what I'm doing. He thought I was nothing but a small girl, but I'm so much more.

I am my father's daughter.

Gripping the tire rod with both hands, I smash it against his head before he even realizes I'm no longer tied up. He groans, then shouts, "Derrick, get back here!"

The passenger falls to the ground, and I reach for Ruby's hand. "We have to run now."

"Dammit!" The driver shouts, as he nears the open back doors. There's no time to waste. I jump out of the van, and we run, Ruby's hand still clasped to mine. I had assumed we were still on the highway, but at some point after dark we must've turned off. This road is two lanes, there are no street lights, no traffic at all. We are in the middle of nowhere, but there is a wooded area to the right. I run.

Ruby's hand slips from mine, but I don't stop to reach back. I'm terrified of slowing down. I hear our abductor, who I now know is Derrick, coming toward us, growling in our direction. "I'm gonna get you, and you're gonna regret it," he shouts.

But he's not going to get me. And I'm not going to regret this. I'm going get as far away from him as possible.

Ruby's hand finds mine again. She's a fast runner. "I don't want to be left alone," she says.

Her voice is laced with a fear I understand. It's the same wrapped around my heart right now. I don't want to die. Not like this. Not now. There's a whole life waiting for me still.

We keep running, our feet snagging on roots as we move without slowing. I have no idea where we are, and I won't be able to gather any sense of direction until morning when light breaks. I just have to stay alive that long.

When we get to a cliff, I hear someone approach. I look at Ruby, and her eyes find mine under the moonlight. "We should go a different way," I say. "Our escape route is cut off."

I would never have chosen to run toward a cliff. But the choice has already been made. There is literally no turning back. Below us is a running river, but I don't know what body of water it is, how deep it might be. If I jump, I have no idea how I'll land.

I see now that the man I hit with the tire iron is on our heels. I suppose they couldn't have both chased us – one of them needed to stay with the other captives in the van.

The light of the moon illuminates him, us. He's bleeding and his eyes are filled with rage as he slowly approaches us. There is a gun in his hand.

"Don't move," he hisses. "I'm going to shoot you if you so much as hesitate."

There's only one choice left. Face my captor or jump into the water below.

I know exactly what my dad would do.

I make a leap, and as I do, I feel Ruby hesitate.

The fall feels like forever. The air in my hair, the terror in my heart. The wind rushing past me, my body feels like a rock but also like a feather. There is pure terror pounding in my heart and I'm scared. So very scared of the fall. I squeeze my eyes shut, hoping for a miracle. As I crash against the icy water, it threatens to turn me into an icicle. My body is heavy, but I refuse to sink.

Gasping, I push myself to the surface. I look up to see where Ruby is and find her still on the top of the cliff, our abductor approaching her. She screams, and I watch as she falls rather than jumps over the edge.

I tread water as I watch Ruby miss the water. Her body lands on the rocky shore. She hits the rocks with a thud that echoes in my ears. She doesn't move. One minute she was alive, holding tight to my hand and now she's gone. The girl with chocolate brown eyes and freckles on her nose, with an innocence masking her bravery, is gone. There is no way she survived that fall. She has been taken from her family forever because of whoever these men are and whatever they want.

Well, they sure as hell aren't getting anything from me.

I refuse to gasp, scream, or cry even though Ruby is gone. I slip under the water, swimming quickly and choosing to let the current carry me downstream. I don't want to bring attention to myself and have the man come down here looking for me. I see him in the darkness, standing high up on the cliff.

I will not be his next target.

2 WILLOW

As I WALK on the campus, I feel a chill in the air. It's November, and the weather has begun to turn. I look up into the sky, and thankfully it's clear and bright blue, no rain clouds in sight. Still, the drop in temperature from 55° to 45° happened quickly. I shove my hands in the pockets of my jacket thinking I should have brought gloves, especially since I have an outdoor lecture today.

Of course, that's nothing new. I teach everything outside on the trails of the beautiful campus of Conifer College. Remembering that I have an extra pair of gloves in my desk drawer, I head to my office.

Once inside the small office space – which is now smaller than ever since I recently traded offices with a fellow professor in exchange for her teaching a class for me last month – I am reminded why I hate being in here for long. It is cramped and has me feeling claustrophobic. Turning on a fluorescent light, I have to squint my eyes in the frosty glow. I shuffle through the few square feet of space and around my desk, moving as fast as possible to get out of here. Even though it is cramped, I use the small space wisely, keeping things tidy in bookshelves and drawers. I pull open my desk drawer to reach for my gloves. As I do, I see my most recent letter from Megan Talbot.

I helped rescue Megan a few months ago after she escaped captivity in the woods near my cabin. She has since moved into her aunt's home in

Chehalis, about ninety minutes away. I unfold and reread a few of the lines she wrote in her slanted ten-year-old handwriting. *I can't wait to see you. You'll get to meet my cat, Sapphire! Her eyes are bright blue.*

Since Megan transitioned to her aunt's home, I've made a concerted effort to be available to them both. It's a big adjustment, but my training as a psychologist has been an opportunity to lend a helping hand while they find their footing as a new family unit. It's not that I am an expert on child psychology, but the trauma that Megan had endured as an involuntary cult member is right up my alley of expertise.

But before I leave town for Chehalis, I have a lecture this morning for my course in the Psychology of Cult Behavior. Out of all the classes I teach, it is by far my favorite. The small cohort of half a dozen students is highly engaged and they always come with interesting questions.

I leave my office, locking the door behind me, and head toward the trail where the class meets. The changing leaves and dewy grass of fall are comforting, but the chill in the air leaves me grateful I chose to grab my gloves. I take in a deep breath of the fresh, cool air, grateful to be back out of that stuffy office space.

Within a few minutes of me getting there, everyone's arrived at the trail head. I look around at the familiar young faces and smile in greeting. They smile back at me with frostbit pink noses and notepads in hand, eager to start absorbing information. "Today is going to be about psychological techniques that cults used to recruit new members."

Caroline – a favorite student of mine – raises her gloved hand. "Like how they initially brainwash them?" she asks.

"Basically, yes. As we have learned over this semester, cults tend to have a mission. And they can be as far-fetched as believing that humans are vessels for the ghosts of brainwashed aliens to the Branch Davidians who later believed he was the Messiah, and that every woman in his fold was one of his spiritual wives." This elicits a quiet chuckle from the class.

We began walking on the trail, the group of us staying close together so we can continue the discussion. "But as crazy as some of those ideas may sound to someone who is outside of the group, once you are recruited, your point of view begins to change as you adopt the group's belief system."

"So what's the pattern?" another student, Sarah, asks.

"Well, there are four basic techniques that are used to draw someone into a cult." We come to a fork on the trail and turn left toward the beach.

"Picking the right target is the first step. College students are easy recruits, but really anyone in an emotionally vulnerable place. Stress in life or someone who feels isolated. Those are the sorts of people looking for a sense of belonging."

Joshua – wearing his signature orange beanie – chimes in. "I said before that cults are looking for people struggling with some sort of mental illness. They're in the most emotionally vulnerable place, right?"

"To an extent," I say. "From a cult's perspective, someone struggling with their mental health would not be an ideal candidate. They could be more unpredictable than someone who's just lonely, and that would move the group further from their goal instead of closer. Healthy people undergoing a stressful situation are the ideal candidate."

As we walk, I describe the step of love-bombing, then isolation, and finally how, after control has been established, they keep it by convincing a new member that they are the best friends they could've ever asked for, and more consistent than family.

"But why would someone believe that this group is going to be better than the family and friends they've always had?" Sarah asks.

"That's a great question." I turn and look at Sarah, putting my hands in my pockets. I stop walking for a second, to really focus on the answer. "It usually involves a combination of love and fear. Those are the two basic emotions and pitting them against one another creates a powerful hold. Manipulation at its finest."

I finish the lecture when we reach the beach. As a group we discuss how members become more and more dependent on the leader the longer they are a part of the group.

There are pine needles covering the ground of the trail, and squirrels skitter past us as we head back to campus. One student asks how you're supposed to break out of a situation that has such a hold on you.

"That's the challenge," I say thoughtfully. "Once our lives become entangled with the group we're involved with, it's hard to see our identity separate from it."

At least, that was the case for me. When I escaped Fountain of Faith, I had no idea who I was. I'm just grateful that there was a still small voice deep within me, whispering that I could find myself again. I feel fortunate, that there was some gut instinct that told me there was more for me than what FoF offered. I know not everyone is so lucky.

As we walk back to the main buildings of campus, past the dining hall and library, I'm approached by a man in his mid-twenties who I've never seen before. "Professor Grace?" He steps toward me on the sidewalk.

"That's me... Can I help you?"

He shrugs, offering me a smile. "I'm Connor McFadden. I just transferred to a psych major after becoming disillusioned with my prelaw classes. I'll be in your class on cult psychology."

"Oh, fantastic. Well I'm sorry that prelaw didn't work out," I say, thinking that it will be funny to tell Malcom that he lost a student to me. "What made you want to change to psych?"

"Honestly, you. I was pushed to make the change when I saw the great things you've been doing."

I chuckle. "Great things? That sounds like a bit of a stretch."

Connor shakes his head. "I've always been fascinated by cult psychology and I heard other students talk about how you're the best in the business, maybe even the country. And then once I saw the article by Veronica Little, about what went down last month with the Carters, I was like okay I gotta transfer. And when I read your latest book, *Tending the Flock*, it was a done deal."

I smile tightly. Veronica Little had written an article featuring Agent Paxton Holt after he took down the cult Harmony, which was near my cabin in the woods. The only reason I was involved in the investigation was because Megan Talbot ended up on my doorstep, trying to escape. Veronica wrote about that situation, then last month she released a new article focusing on Amy Carter, the heiress of the tech giant Jackson Carter who had been kidnapped and brainwashed by her captors – which was the second case I helped Agent Holt solve.

"Veronica really does like to sensationalize things," I reply succinctly. "I'm not usually rubbed the wrong way by people I don't know, but Veronica tends to over dramatize everything. And I don't know who that serves other than herself. Certainly not the victims."

"Yeah, I thought so too," Connor says with a smile. "She seemed set on making Amy look like a fool instead of the target. That's something I'm never going to be okay with."

I nod slowly, appreciating his take. Connor has a generous smile. He's taller than me and well-spoken. "I look forward to seeing you in class next week," I say.

He nods. "You know, I was wondering, since I'm coming in late to the semester if there's any way I could come by during office hours to catch up on some of the course content? I'm especially interested in cult conditioning. I know that was relevant to the situation with the Carters, and if you have any lecture notes or course materials that I could look at, that'd be great."

Amy Carter wasn't just kidnapped. She'd been conditioned and quickly fell in love with her kidnapper. A classic Stockholm situation where she ended up working with the person holding her hostage instead of the detectives assigned to the case.

"That sounds great, but I'm not holding my office hours today. I have a prior commitment. But how about next Tuesday before class? We can meet in my office then."

Connor smiles warmly and agrees to the plan. Then since I'm already outside and near the parking lot, I head to my car. I'm going to see Megan Talbot and meet her new cat Sapphire.

3 AGENT HOLT

RUBY FALLON
  Chelsea Hammond
  Rachel Presley
  Tori Sinclair
  Brittney Baker

These girls – all thirteen years old, all taken from Seattle neighborhoods – all went missing the same night. The team of FBI agents searching for them are gathered in the meeting room at the agency. I'm debriefing them on the current state of the investigation, but right now, we have limited leads.

"None of the girls listed have any history of running away, though they all look similar if you compare their most recent photographs. Tall for their age, long dark hair, and brown eyes. After speaking with the parents, it's clear they have no overlap in relationships. They all go to different schools and none are connected through a specific interest or hobby."

The atmosphere in the room is tense. One missing girl is tragic enough. But five? That's untenable.

"We do have phone records," Agent Gonzales says, "and we're going through messages to see if there is some connection between them, but as of now, nothing has been substantiated." Gonzales hesitated. "We're continuing to investigate this as a mass kidnapping."

· · ·

A whiteboard at the front of the room reveals the information we have at hand. When I look at the images, it's strange, but I note a resemblance to Willow Grace. She's tall and has long dark hair too. But I put her out of my mind. I have to focus on the case.

"Of course I know what we're all thinking. That perhaps this is more than a kidnapping," I say. "No one wants a serial killer on the loose, and as of now we've yet to recover a body. Unless the situation changes, we're not going to take a leap there. Not yet."

"The story will make national headlines unless the girls are found in a few hours," Agent Bolles says, he's an older man with close-cropped black hair and a mustache.

"The good news is, we do have one lead," I say. "A witness saw a white van around the time Brittney Baker went missing. There was a large dent on the side door."

"This whole situation is a shit show," Agent Gonzales says, shaking his head. Gonzales is a younger agent, with a deep voice; when he speaks people pay attention. It's a good skill for an agent.

"I'm not listening to anything negative right now. We need to stay positive, and believe the girls will be found, and that they will all be alive when they are rescued. We're not going to become discouraged. We're going to stay focused. I have faith in you to do your job."

The agents nod collectively and move to stand. I join them in exiting the room. We all have work to do.

When I get in the hall, my phone starts to buzz. It's Detective Smith from the Seattle Police Department. We worked together last month on the Jackson Carter case. He's a solid guy, and shockingly enough, I enjoyed working alongside him. It wasn't what I'd expected when we first met, but over the week of the investigation, I realized we worked together really well.

I take the call. "Hey, Smith, what's up?"

"I'm working the missing girls' case on the local end. I wanted to touch base and see if you have any leads."

"No shit, I didn't realize that." Learning that Smith is working the same case is good news. "One lead. A witness spotted a white van around where Brittney Baker was taken, over in Magnolia. I'm thinking we can get some footage pulled up from local gas stations and traffic lights."

"I'll update patrol and see what they can find, too."

"It's good to hear we'll be working together," I tell him.

Smith chuckles. "Yeah, especially since this might be my last case."

I laugh, surprised since Smith is so good at his job. Good reminder of why I like the guy. "Really? What's the plan?"

"My wife wants to move to Nashville. See if she can really make a go at it. And you know me, I'm ready for a change."

"Well, in the meantime, you're stuck with me." I chuckle and so does Smith. "I'll make sure to keep you posted if any new leads develop."

"Same. I just really hope we find these girls before the clock runs out."

I run a hand over my jaw. Forty-seven percent of missing children are found within three hours. This is hour eighteen. If they're not found within the next seventy-two hours, there's a sixty percent chance they will never be recovered.

Every minute counts.

4 CHELSEA

I WAKE with my body pressed against the trunk of a cedar tree. Its long heavy limbs sheltered me from the night sky. My clothing is still damp from the swim last night. I'd moved downstream, as far from my abductors as possible. The sound of Ruby's body hitting the rocky shore is still fresh in my mind. I was hoping to wake up this morning and it'd all have been a dream.

But it's not a dream. I am lost in the woods, far from home, hungry and frozen.

Tears fill my eyes as I consider what my dad must be thinking right now. I'm not trying to be too dramatic, but I also know I am his whole wide world. After mom died, I became his sun, his moon, his stars. And that's a lot of pressure.

It also means I'm loved more than anyone else.

And gosh, the idea of him being in pain right now, worried and scared, hurts my heart. I blink my eyes quickly, wanting the tears to fade. Knowing I need to be strong. Last night it was so cold and dark, and I didn't have it within me to try to make a fire, but now I can. I start to work on gathering dry kindling and sticks. One good thing is that my dad is smart. The smartest man I know. He's an Army Ranger, and he's spent his whole life teaching me how to survive.

It was our thing. Father-daughter bonding. Mom would go on trips to visit her cousins or her college roommates, and we would go camping. In the woods, just like this. And not fancy camping. Dad would have me compete against him to see who could make a fire the fastest. Who could catch the first trout, who could set up a tent in under a minute. The older I got, the closer we became as competitors.

But Dad's not out here right now setting up a survival course. Trying to test my skills. I am here all by myself. And I have to remember the things he taught me. I gather bark, the driest pieces I can find, and I begin grinding the sticks together, working hard until my fingers are numb, until they ache, until the wood begins to smoke. And then I blow, willing it to life, urging a flicker to grow to a flame.

When it does, a thrill runs over me. I did it. I made that happen. And no matter what happens next, I know Dad would be proud.

The sun is just barely up. I have no idea if it's seven or eight or nine in the morning, but the fire is burning, and I warm my hands over it. When I was little, Dad and I would always watch that reality TV show *Survivor*, sometimes laughing at the people who couldn't make a fire, even with flint. Dad always said I would never be that girl. I would always be able to stay warm.

I close my eyes and send a silent prayer his way. And then I send another, this time to my mom. I'm not sure I believe in God or angels or heaven or any of that, but I do believe that Mom loves me. And that she's looking out for me, wherever she might be right now. "Mom," I whisper to the sky. "I'm scared, please keep me safe, and keep the other girls safe too. And Ruby ... if you find her up there, can you give her a hug?"

I'm not sure I totally believe in the idea of miracles, but I'm alive, and Ruby isn't, and something about that makes me want to fight for a second chance. It feels like dumb luck, that I'm sitting here, getting warm, and she's lying on those rocks, growing cold.

As I shove my hands in my pockets, wanting to stay as warm as possible, my stomach growls. I'm so hungry. The men certainly didn't feed us when they shoved us into their van. My throat is parched too, but that's something I can take care of at least. I walk to the stream closest to where I camped out, and I dip my hands in the water, needing to drink.

I scan the horizon, and I see nothing and no one. No smoke in the distance or any house nestled in a hill. I'm utterly alone. But I need to move, find a road, a sign of life. Maybe if I'm lucky, I'll find a hiker. Someone else has got to be out here.

A noise crackles and echoes through the woods. Not the birds singing or the leaves rustling in the wind. Footsteps.

For a moment, my heart hitches up high. With hope. Maybe someone is here to rescue me.

But then I hear the voice in the distance. A voice I recognized. "She can't be far," Derrick shouts, presumably to whomever he's walking with.

The man who'd abducted me. My whole body shivers from cold and fear. I don't want to end up like Ruby.

I need to stay alive. If I die, Dad will break.

Dipping my hands back in the water, I toss as much as I can over the fire. I repeat this until I've fully doused the flames. Without looking back, I cross a shallow point in the stream, knowing I need to send myself in the opposite direction of the men's voices.

The scary part is I don't know if I'm sending myself deeper into the forest and further from the road, or if I'm going to be closer to home.

5 WILLOW

AFTER LEAVING CAMPUS, I drive straight to Chehalis to see Megan. I haven't seen her since she moved to her aunt's home, and I'm hopeful that I find her in a positive mental state.

Her childhood was so difficult. After being kidnapped at a young age, she'd spent the next several years in a cult named Harmony, where she was conditioned to believe the world was dangerous and that the leaders of the congregation were the only ones who could be trusted.

On top of that, she witnessed her brother Kevin's murder. And Kevin had been her closest ally in the world. While her aunt is a safe haven, they'd just met for the first time a month ago, when Megan moved here. It's so much change, so much new, and the girl at the tender age of ten will be processing everything for a long time.

A month ago, when I spoke to Megan's Aunt Cory, she mentioned how much television Megan had been watching after school and how she'd been relying on junk food for comfort. Her aunt had been worried, thinking this behavior was problematic for a young child. She thought Megan should be outside, meeting kids in the neighborhood and playing or riding a bike. But I reminded her that Megan was processing a lot and just going to school all day was an expense of energy she wasn't used to.

She'd grown up in a small community, whose members were controlling and dangerous, all while creating a false sense of shelter and safety. Going to public school was a huge adjustment and at the end of the day I could understand why binging Netflix would be all she could handle. She was exhausted. And although Oreos and boxed macaroni and cheese aren't a long-term solution for meals, I assured her aunt that for now, it was fine. Megan just needed to get through these next few weeks and find her footing.

Eventually, she would come into her own skin, and she'd be outside getting fresh air and riding bikes. When winter came, she'd be building snowmen at the park and grabbing cocoa at friends' houses.

A month has passed, and I'm excited to share some more ideas of how Megan could move forward in her new life with her aunt. I'm not exactly sure how receptive Megan is going to be of them, though.

Change is hard, but in most cases, it's essential for growth. I am choosing to hold onto faith that Megan will be able to rise to the occasion.

When I pull up to the house, I'm happy to see it has a well-maintained yard and a clean front porch., it gives me a sense that Cory is a conscientious human, who will do more than the bare minimum when it comes to parenting Megan.

I get out of my car and walk to the door, then knock on it. Megan pulls it open, beaming. A small kitten sits in the crook of her left arm. I smile, reaching out to give Megan a hug.

"This must be Sapphire," I say as Megan squeezes me tight, the kitten jumping from her arms and skittering down the hallway.

Megan beams up at me as we step apart. "You made it."

"Of course I did," I say. "Did you think I wasn't going to come?"

Megan shrugs. "I don't know. You never know who you can count on."

I see Cory coming from the kitchen, wiping her hands on a hand towel. She smiles at me.

"Well, I'm not going to let you down, Megan," I say, "and I'm sorry that that's been your experience so far in life."

Megan shrugs, running back down the hall to find her kitten.

Cory welcomes me with a hug. "It's so good to see you again," she says.

I smile warmly. "It's great to see you too. Your house smells incredible. Is that a candle?"

She laughs. "No, it's a pumpkin pie. I've been trying to perfect a recipe for Thanksgiving. I want to spend the next few weeks getting this meal right." She closes the front door behind me and I follow her into the kitchen. She begins opening cupboards and slows for a moment. "I just want it to be perfect for Megan."

"You know, nobody needs perfect." I rest a gentle hand on her shoulder. "People just need real, especially kids. Don't put pressure on yourself for making everything just so."

She sighs though and asks me if I'd like a cup of coffee. I glance over at the pot and see it's already brewed.

"That sounds delicious," I tell her.

Cory reaches for a carton of cream in the fridge and carries it over to the counter. Before pouring us each a mug of coffee, she indicates that I sit at the table in the corner and then hands me a full mug. "Megan," she calls out, "do you want some pie?"

Megan comes back in with Sapphire in her arms. It's a pretty little kitten with the promised bright blue eyes. "Of course I want pie," Megan says.

She sits down at the table opposite me. Cory brings us our slices of pie and Megan a glass of milk. It warms my heart to see how well this girl is being cared for. I know her aunt had lost her husband not too long ago and she works from home a few days a week, which means she has a lot of time to devote to Megan.

I know many children are not so lucky. They are put in the foster care system, and they struggle through school. But sitting here, eating this pie, and drinking this coffee fills me with hope I didn't know I needed. Many of my private clients – all leaving tragic situations where they've been brainwashed in cults – struggle for years to find any sort of solid foundation for their new lives. I sometimes forget that there can be happily ever afters. But seeing Megan here reminds me that not everything in life is so grim. Some things can be great.

"So," I say, " how are things going?"

Megan shrugs, looking over at Cory. "Pretty good I think," Megan tells me. "In science class, we're talking about biomes. Do you know what that is? It's like all different sorts of areas in the world. Like we're living in a biome right now."

I smile, listening to her explain the different biomes. I can tell her mind is like a sponge. After years of a very controlled curriculum at Harmony, it's clear her mind is expanding for the first time in her life, entertaining new ideas, and considering different possibilities. It warms my heart to listen to her.

I look over at Cory and smile. "You must be very proud. Megan seems really excited about school."

Cory nods at me. "Yes," she says, "but I've been trying to see if Megan would like to join a club or some sort of activity. It's kind of just school and home right now." She looks over at Megan.

Megan looks down at the pie, picking at it with her fork.

"It's not that I want Megan to go, go, go," her aunt continues, "but I would like the idea of her meeting some kids her own age and testing out a hobby or a sport. There's a gymnastics studio not far from here. And I read about some art classes downtown."

I look over at Megan. "Do either of those things sound fun to you?" I ask.

"I don't know." She lifts her shoulders in a shrug. "I like it here. I don't know why I have to go anywhere else."

Cory sighs. "It's not that you have to go somewhere else. It's just, I don't know, I want you to have every opportunity imaginable, Megan. I want you to feel like you have a childhood."

I take a moment to think about how I want to phrase things, not wanting to lose Megan when I just got here. "The thing is, keeping busy after you've gone through a really hard season can be more important than you think," I tell her. "I know you've had a month where you've been able to take things slow, but playing with friends, or trying something new, could give you confidence you've yet to experience, Megan." I let her process for a moment and I take a bite of pie before continuing. It tastes how a candle smells. "Another idea is you and your aunt could do an activity together."

Cory's eyes widen at the suggestion, clearly not having thought of it herself.

"Maybe there's somewhere you could volunteer," I add. "Sometimes doing things for other people helps us process the things we've gone through ourselves."

Cory nods slowly. "You know, there is a soup kitchen, and I saw a friend post on Facebook how they were looking for volunteers for Thanksgiving dinner."

Megan looks over at her. "What does that mean? What's a soup kitchen?"

"It's a place where people who are un-housed can go get a meal, but when there's a holiday, it's an extra special meal. Like a Thanksgiving meal."

Megan nods. "And you just go and help people who don't have houses, people who live out on the street?"

Cory nods. "Yeah. And, you know, I've been kind of worried about how Thanksgiving would go. Maybe it would be fun to go to the shelter and help other people?"

Megan smiles softly. "I'd like that. I wouldn't have to talk a lot, would I?"

"Is talking to people overwhelming?" I speak as gently as possible, wanting her to feel free of judgement so she can express herself.

Megan shrugs. "Kind of. I don't want to hang out with kids my age because what if they ask where I came from? What am I supposed to say? It's weird."

"Do you feel like that at school?" I ask. "Do you eat with other kids at lunch?"

Megan shakes her head. "No. I eat in the library. The teacher said I can."

"I'm glad you've found a place where you can eat that feels safe. But, you know, everyone's gone through hard things. It's just different hard things. I think you might be surprised that some of the kids you're in school with, that you're in class with might have faced really difficult things themselves."

"Really?" Megan twists her lips. "I don't want people to make fun of me."

"Oh, Megan," I say, "nobody's going to make fun of you. But maybe finding people who have gone through similar things as you have will help you. We could look into a support group for kids your age."

We all finish our pie and I help clear the table. Megan has once again gone off chasing Sapphire. I finish the conversation with Cory. "I wasn't trying to interject too much," I tell her.

She shakes her head. "No. I'm glad you said something. I think it's a great idea to go to a soup kitchen, and a really good idea for Megan to meet other kids who've faced hardship. I didn't even think about finding a support group for kids like her."

"Well, it wouldn't be exactly her," I clarify. "Megan's situation is pretty unique, but there are trauma support groups. Not sure if she would be up for it quite yet though."

When I tell Megan and her aunt goodbye, they each give me a big hug and wave me out the door. I give another wave when I get to my car. Driving away, I feel a renewed sense of purpose. I can help people. I decide then that, no matter what comes my way, I'm going to dive in with open arms. Because even though the real world can be a terrifying place, the scariest part of all is going at it alone.

6 AGENT HOLT

THE OFFICE I work out of is crowded, loud, has terrible lightening, and even worse coffee. And I'm making a mess of the blueberry muffin I got at the corner coffee shop. There are crumbs all over my already messy desk. If Willow saw my work space, she'd make a few choice comments. She keeps everything tidy. And while my home is cleaned regularly by a very helpful housekeeper, my cubicle? Not so much.

Smith calls again. I pick up the phone immediately. Maybe he's got a lead. "What's up?"

"Word is there's a local gang running girls. Just heard it from the Narcotics Crime Detective. I put out feelers to my snitches earlier, asked if anyone knew if something sketchy was up."

"Shit. Anything about a white van?"

Smith clicks his tongue. "I'm not sure, but the street detective is trying to hammer down a location. I think it might be somewhere in Seattle off exit one forty-five."

I press my lips together, thinking. "That up by University of Washington?"

"Yeah."

"Want to meet there?"

"Actually," Smith says, "I'm pretty close to the agency downtown. Are you in the office?"

"Yeah. "A few minutes later, Smith and I are in his car. We're rolling toward the neighborhood where the gang is known to operate. The tension in the car's stuffy air is palpable. I'm cracking my knuckles and he's tapping the steering wheel. Neither of us speak much. Things feel off.

"You okay?" I ask him.

He shrugs. "I don't know. Something about this feels different than other cases."

"Because it came in pretty quick, word about the gang?"

"Yeah. And knowing that they're running girls is" – he takes a breath and shakes his head – "shitty. I hate hearing that kind of stuff going down. Kids should not be sex trafficked."

"Damn, I know," I say.

It's the crap part of the job. This work is difficult and demanding. Not just physically, but mentally. Emotionally. It can mess you up to think about how terrible people can be, and how easily they can use, hurt, and destroy others. But right now, I can't get into some existential crisis with Smith. We need to find out if this gang is the same one who took these thirteen-year-old girls. The clock is ticking. They need to get home.

We pull up alongside a patrol officer, and Smith rolls to a stop, not even bothering to put the car in park. The officer tells Smith that the local cops have been alerted to stay clear of this area so we don't spook the potential suspects. "Roger that," Smith says before pulling away.

The street is in a rough area, one I would never go to if not on assignment. If girls have been kept somewhere here, it is goings to be a sad situation, no way around it. Pedestrians eye us, or scurry away. A half dozen unhoused people are under awnings with their possessions.

"What do we know about the gang?" I ask him as he drives to a discreet place to park.

"They're making their moves running drugs and guns," Smith says. "But my source said they made a move into trafficking girls in the last few months."

"Shit. And no one's been able to bust them yet?"

"Nope. They've got to be a dangerous crew, and if they have some narcotic ring along with buying and selling guns, it could get ugly real fast, especially if we're trying to take what they *think* they own."

"And by *what they think they own* ... you mean children?" I say, my whole body lit up with anger. I control it, because I have been trained to keep my emotions in check, but my body responds, nonetheless. This group of men needs to pay. More than that, they deserve to suffer. "Damn, I'm glad you spoke to the detectives who knew about this. So there could be a way to put a stop to this."

"Yeah," Smith says. "Thing is, I'm not really looking for a showdown. My wife will kill me if I die."

I snort at that. From what I understand, he and his wife are figuring their shit out. She wants to move to Nashville and Smith dying might ruin her plans.

Sitting in Smith's beat-up slick top, a detective car with a low profile, allows us to creep into the neighborhoods where lookouts are everywhere. No one will know who we are or see us coming. We pull over to the side of a road where the gang we are looking for has been seen dealing. While we wait, we catch up.

Smith tells me his wife is headed east to record an album.

"Really?" I say. "Nashville then?"

He nods. "Yeah. I'm going to take early retirement and go into business on my own, cashing out will help fund her dreams. Mine too."

I look over at him, surprised. "I was hoping you might want to become an FBI agent."

Smith chuckles. "Nah. That's not for me. I'm sick of corporate."

"Being a police officer or an FBI agent is not a corporate job."

"Maybe," he says, "but it locks me into a life I don't want. I'm sick of this shit. I want to be my own boss."

"So what does that look like exactly?" I ask him.

"I think I'm going to be a private investigator."

As we talk, we keep looking out the window, scanning for anyone walking across the street. Anything suspect.

"An investigator might be useful to me," I tell him. I look over at him and grin.

"How so?"

"We could work together, but you could skirt the procedural hold backs that are typical with a regular police investigation."

"I see," Smith says with a laugh. "So you think my choice of changing careers is going to work in your favor?"

"I guess not if you live in Nashville," I say with a laugh.

He chuckles and shakes his head. "I don't want to move to Nashville, but Natalie's gonna go there and make an album. See what can come of it."

"She pretty talented?" I ask him.

He nods. "She can't get many gigs here in Seattle and the girl's got big dreams."

"So she could go to Nashville and make an album, get a record deal, go on tour," I suggest. "Meanwhile, you can stay here and be a private investigator to help me out."

Smith chuckles. "Wow, you came up with a whole life plan for me pretty damn fast. Considering Willow gave me some free therapy last time I saw her, I owe both of you guys."

"You owe me nothing," I say. "The fact we get along is enough of a win. Usually I don't get along with my coworkers. At least not like this."

"Hey," Smith says, turning up the radio when we hear chatter picking up. A street detective is telling us that his snitch just came out of the target location. "Did he find girls inside?" Smith asks.

"Yeah. All of them look to be underage and drugged."

"Damn," he mutters, tension lining his voice. "I'll inform the tactical commander that we've met the warrant's trigger point. It's time to execute the search warrant."

Usually, a search warrant would be sanctioned by a prosecutor and a judge after establishing enough probable cause and gathering all pieces of the puzzle. Getting the sign-off when teetering on the fringe of PC, while still waiting on a specific set of circumstances to validate suspicion, is what's known as an anticipatory search warrant. Used sparingly – and typically on cases where immediate police intervention is needed to prevent the destruction of crucial evidence or potential physical harm to innocent third parties – its approval now couldn't be more important.

The anticipatory search warrant remains inactive until a trigger is met. For us, the triggering event was the informant's tip-off that the girls were held inside. This decisive piece of information, like the last piece of a puzzle, lends credence to our suspicions, transforming them into probable cause. The anticipatory search warrant, secured earlier, now roars into effect, giving us the green light to storm the location.

Deep breath. Slow exhale.

It's go time.

Before I exit the vehicle, I send a quick text to Willow. *Sorry,* I say. *I have to cancel dinner for tonight. Big case going down. Call you later.*

"What?" Smith asks, looking over at me. "Who are you texting at a time like this?"

I slip my phone back in my pocket. "Willow," I say.

"Willow." Smith shakes his head as he turns off his car. "You and her, is it a thing yet?"

I sigh. "Not even close."

And since I just canceled on her for tonight, I'm guessing it's going to stay in the *I don't know* zone for quite some time.

7 WILLOW

I'T'S late afternoon when I get home from visiting Megan and her aunt in Chehalis. The drive wasn't long and somehow, I avoided traffic. When I pull up the long driveway to my house, I am immediately overwhelmed with a sense of gratitude. I'm so thankful to have this pocket of the world that is just my own. And after a long day of work and an emotional conversation with Megan, I am more thankful than ever to have a place that is just mine.

Growing up, I didn't have such a place. I shared everything. My room, my bed, my body. Nothing was just my own. Nothing was sacred. Now, I'm overwhelmingly protective of the life I have carved out for myself. I know that makes it more difficult for me to let people in – I've created a literal wall around me, a security system that surrounds my property, that keeps out any intruder, but also keeps me safe, tucked inside.

I'm trying to loosen up, to change. Meeting Holt has done wonders for me. Inviting him into my home several times now in and of itself has meant I'm becoming more vulnerable, more open to sharing my life with people, with him. We have a date tonight and I'm looking forward to it. He'll come over when he gets off work, which will probably be pretty late, maybe eight o'clock.

When I get my car parked, I step up to my place, two bags of groceries balanced in my arms. After unlocking the door, I re-secure my surveillance system. If there had been any alerts of activity on my property throughout the day, I would've been notified on my phone. Not even a rogue deer or raccoon set off any alarms, which does happen from time to time. Still, as I walk into my home, I always make sure that everything is undisturbed, that no one's in any of the rooms. Before inspecting the other rooms, I set the groceries on the kitchen counter, then continue my reconnaissance. I check both bedrooms, and then the porch off the kitchen. Lastly, I use the custom design key on my key ring to unlock the padlock on the door to my office. I know a padlock can be shot through pretty easily, or someone could bring bolt cutters and get through, but it's not about the literal security this padlocked door offers. It's the idea that the things inside are locked away, kept safe. My office doesn't just hold my current works or projects in progress.

It is also where I keep all of my most private memories. Documents of my past, photographs that show the kind of woman I used to be when I wore a long dress, my hair in one braid, my face free of makeup, and my heart so damn heavy it felt impossible to carry most days. I was worried that I'd lost all of those memorabilia when the police department went through my office a few months ago.

When I was part of the investigation into Megan's kidnapping, there was a moment when I was being investigated as the kidnapper. During that time, the police ransacked my home, and disturbed my most valuable possessions. I was able to recover everything, though now the memories are buried even deeper than ever in the closet of my office. I don't feel any need to sort through them or bring that baggage back up.

Still, it's on my mind as I make myself a cup of tea, preparing for my video call with Linda Benedict. She and I both come from situations where our behavior was controlled, and our personal freedom was restricted. She lived in a polygamist group where she had no rights, fought for her survival, and had to take massive risks to escape and give herself a chance at a new future. We've been having a weekly call as she's processed her trauma.

With my tea in hand, I enter my office and boot up my computer. As I wait a few minutes before the meeting, I look at the to-do list that I created yesterday. I already checked off getting groceries for my dinner date with Holt. I grabbed lettuce, blue cheese, tomatoes, and flank steak on my way home from Megan's place. The other item on the list besides this therapy session is to make an appointment to get my hair done and go to a mall to buy some clothes. Alternately, I wrote that I could get some online shopping done. I twist my lips as I look at my list. The phone call and the grocery shopping were easy, but giving myself a little bit of a makeover feels more ambitious.

I've never been one for overanalyzing my appearance. I'm pretty no-nonsense. But lately I've been feeling frumpy. Maybe it's because I am 36 and getting closer to 40 than 30. I want to present myself to the world as I want to be seen, and as I consider that, I realize maybe I am growing up in ways I hadn't realized. Maybe I'm elevating myself, seeing myself in a more polished way than I ever have before, and that brings a small smile to my face – I am full of hope. Hope that we – me, Linda, Megan – can continue to grow and change and evolve into the best versions of ourselves.

I hear the reminder alert on my phone that I set for the Zoom call, and I click to enter the room. Linda is already there waiting, her black hair streaked with natural gray. Her eyes are warm and she has a smile on her face, which gives me an instant sense of relief. Sometimes she's crying before we even exchange hellos.

"It's so great to see you," I tell her.

She smiles back at me. "You too, Willow."

"You look great," I say. "You're feeling good?"

"I'm feeling incredible. I think those tips you gave me last time about mindfulness really work. I downloaded that app you suggested, and I've been doing the daily meditations."

"And what do you think of those?" I ask.

Her eyes widen slightly. "Honestly, I thought it was going to be a little bit too woo-woo for me, like maybe even triggering if it was too much like prayer because that was so much of my past, but it didn't feel like that at all. It was like giving myself a chance to just turn off my mind and stop replaying my memories and instead just be present."

I chuckle slightly. "I think that's the point. Meditation is a powerful tool and even if you do it for just a few minutes a day, it can change your entire mindset. And don't forget, it's not about length of time that you meditate. It's about consistency. Doing it five minutes a day every day is better than doing it for, say, an hour once a week."

Linda nods. "I wish I had known about meditation after I escaped the first time."

I nod, remembering elements of Linda's story. She'd escaped once but had let down her guard and was found after a relentless search for her. She hadn't been prepared to survive on her own, and after a time, she gave up.

"Don't beat yourself up about that," I tell her. "You did the best you could with the skills that you had in the moment."

"I still look over my shoulder every day," she says.

"Anxiety is going to be a part of your story for a while, but eventually I know you're going to be able to release that." I say those things to her even though I haven't been able to put them into practice myself. But Linda's experience definitely parallels my own. Meditation changed the game for me, and I know, one day, I'll be able to release the anxiety surrounding my past.

We continue our phone call and I give Linda space to process her week. She's got a job interview at a corporate warehouse where she could be a packer, and the hours would be a lot better than her shifts at the fast food joint. The fact that she is looking for new ways to improve her life with her employment is another positive. She's not going to settle. Not anymore.

"I'm really proud of you," I tell her as we end the call. "And I'm looking forward to hearing how the job interview goes. I know you'll do great. Just bring that smile with you and you'll hit it out of the park."

When we get off the call, I check my phone and I see that I've received a text from Holt. I frown, realizing I missed it while I was conducting my therapy session. The message is simple but demoralizing. Holt can't make it to dinner tonight. He's working a heavy case and won't be able to get out here.

Rain check? he texts.

Determined not to get down, I give him a quick thumbs up before returning to my computer screen. I guess I'm not going to need to wait to eat. My steak salad will be for one.

And while I enjoy my meal, I suppose I can do that online shopping.

8 CHELSEA

It doesn't take long until I'm far enough away for me to no longer hear the men's voices, but I keep walking faster and faster. I'm scared to run. I don't want to trip and fall over any of the roots on the forest floor, but I want to find a highway, a road, a lamppost, some guide.

I want to get home. I want to see my dad. I don't want to cry.

I pause at a river, and I realize that I must have gone in some sort of circle, unless there's another river or a stream. Tears prick my eyes. "Stay brave, Chelsea. Don't fall apart now." I wipe away my tears. I want to hold my myself together because if I start crying, I might never stop, and if I stop moving altogether, I'll never be found. And right now, all I want is to get out of these woods, out of these cold clothes, and have my dad wrap his arms around me. I want him to give me a hug that feels like safety. A hug that feels like home.

I kneel at the river and cup my hands in the water. I'm parched, my throat so dry it hurts to swallow. It takes a while to get enough in my mouth, but I keep drinking until my throat is no longer dry. Then I splash water on my face, not because I care about getting cleaned up, but because I need to stay awake and alert. The ice-cold water stings my skin and pumps my adrenaline. The wilderness is expansive. I hear animals around me, but I can't really see them. Everything is starting to feel blurry as exhaustion washes over me. Birds overhead wrestle in the trees, and there's a scampering in some brush nearby.

I swallow away any fear I have, even though when I hear the howl of a coyote, there's no sense in being naive any longer. I have to find shelter, somewhere to sleep. It's been a long day and I'm starving. I've been moving for hours. My whole body is tired.

I look up to the sky saying a prayer to a God I've never believed in, that the rain stays away because if it starts to fall... No, I can't think like that. My chest is tight as a knot of worry wraps around my heart.

I don't want to freeze to death out here. I get spooked when the coyote howls again, and maybe I'm losing it, but I swear it's closer. I start to run through the woods, even though I said I wouldn't, but I'm scared. I'm scared of that animal finding me, taking me down. Now the tears are impossible to keep at bay and as I run, I trip. I fall, my knees screaming as they scrape against a rock. My arm hooks on a branch. I tug at it, my coat ripping as I try to get myself free. My hands are bloody. I squeeze my eyes shut. "Don't be dramatic, Chelsea. You can do this. You can do hard things." The pep talk feels futile though. I run my hand over my ripped jacket. It's red. I remember buying it at REI with my dad last winter.

I haven't had much of a growth spurt so it still fits, and he told me to get a bright red one because he wouldn't lose me in it. I don't think he was talking about me getting lost in the woods. I think he was thinking about us being in a crowd, going into Seattle and being around tourists, wanting to always be able to spot me. I think I would've gone with a green, personally. But I let him buy the red for me anyways because I like the idea of my dad wanting to make sure he could always keep an eye on me, that he could always find me. Right now, I just want to be found.

The coyote howls again. Three times is one time too many, so I start to run once more, quickly deciding I'm an idiot because I don't see how fast the hill slopes and I roll down it, slamming hard against a tree at the bottom.

My whole body barrels into it at full force. I scream out loud, unable to hold back my cry. "Oww," I gasp. My eyes close as I brace through the pain, and I try to remember the ice-cold water I splashed against my face.

"Stay alert, Chelsea. Stay alive." But it's hard. My eyes close, and when I wake a moment later, I can't remember what happened. I realize it's only been a few moments based on sun's position. The sky is the same. But it takes me a second to remember the hill and falling down it and the tree, and so I begin to crawl. Hours tick by and the air becomes frigid. My body trembles as I attempt to make my way through the forest floor.

My bloody hands move slowly, my busted-up knees move, and my mind tries to process everything as I try to clear my vision. In the distance, I see a small outcropping of rocks that could work as a makeshift shelter for the night. It's not a cave exactly, but I reject the idea as the last thing I want to do is be in an animal's den when he comes back for dinner.

The air and forest floor are too damp for a fire, and I don't have the energy to try to rub two sticks together. Instead, I wrap my arms around myself, huddling against a rock, tight in a corner. The moon is out, high and heavy in the sky. A beacon of light.

My dad's looking up at that same moon right now. That should give me more hope than it does – that moon shines down across everyone in this whole planet, and out of 8 billion people, maybe it's crazy to think my dad can find me.

My head throbs and I run my hand to the back of it, where a lump is already forming. I wince as I touch it. When I look at my fingers, they're red with blood. I try to take a deep, deep breath in and out as panic presses tight against my chest and tears streak my cheeks.

I close my eyes, scared and wondering if I'll ever escape the nightmare I've found myself in.

9 AGENT HOLT

WE HAVEN'T LEFT the street where we are hoping to rescue the kidnapped girls. Smith and I observe with anticipation as the SWAT team swiftly maneuvers into position, their movements synchronized and precise. The tactical unit employs a BearCat, a robust and heavily armored vehicle, to approach the target location. Its purpose is to ensure the team can safely advance while minimizing any potential harm.

Surrounding the target, the SWAT team members are stationed at various exit points, covering each. Although their numbers may be few, the team is determined to not make any errors in this critical operation.

In conjunction with SWAT's efforts, the patrol division establishes a comprehensive outer perimeter, effectively sealing off the surrounding streets within a one-block radius. This ensures minimal opportunity for any civilian interference, safeguarding both the public and the integrity of the operation. This outer perimeter serves an additional crucial role: in the event that a suspect manages to breach the inner perimeter, it acts as a secondary line of defense. The significance of this arrangement cannot be overstated, as the last thing we want is an unforeseen individual jeopardizing the entire operation by entering or exiting the building at the wrong moment. The level of planning and coordination invested thus far demands flawless execution.

As I turn my attention towards the entry team, comprised of seven highly skilled individuals, I notice them stacked together, forming a cohesive unit. After careful consideration, we have determined that the main entrance offers the most optimal access point. The team remains poised and prepared for the imminent entry.

I glance at Smith and sense the weight of the situation weighing heavily upon him. While we have confronted intense scenarios together in the past, the presence of the young girls inside the building sets this apart. Their families are anguished, desperately hoping for their safe return. These girls were forcibly taken from their homes, amplifying the urgency and gravity of our mission.

Ensuring the survival and safe extraction of these innocent lives has become our paramount objective, without a shadow of a doubt.

The protocol is to call out to the suspects inside using the BearCat's PA system. The leader of the entry team makes the calls, but there's no response from within. I glance up to the roof of an apartment building across the street and spot a sniper team. On the radio, the sniper team lead calls out that there is movement in one of the windows. Smith and I have our hands on our hips, guns at the ready. It's not that we're about to start shooting, but hell could break lose any minute. Sometimes the sniper teams will use drones, but it's not necessary right now. And while a chemical agent like gas is another option, because of the number of innocents inside, it's the last thing we want to use.

Feels like we're waiting for ages. In reality, it's only minutes.

Eventually, the SWAT commander has his team make several more attempts, and uses the PA system to call out for them to release the girls. But when we don't hear back from the suspects, the order to force entry is given.

Damn it. I didn't want it to come to this. I don't want any armed thugs to amp up the probability of injury or death. It's a high-risk operation and I don't want anyone to die. To compensate for this threat, the SWAT team uses speed, surprise, and violence of action. It's the best way to overwhelm the enemy and reduce potential harm on both sides, for both the suspect and the cops.

The team needs to utilize a breacher to initiate a tactical entry. They bring in a heavy 60-pound ram, applying controlled force to crush the door. I'm relieved they chose this method, as resorting to explosive breaching could pose serious risks of injury.

Right now, my primary concern is the safe recovery of those girls. I yearn to witness the sheer relief in their eyes, knowing they will be reunited with their families tonight.

Once the breacher successfully clears the door, the next team member in the tactical stack swiftly deploys a flashbang. The team braces themselves for the deafening sound and blinding light emitted by the device, effectively disorienting anyone in close proximity for approximately fifteen seconds. Frankly, every time I witness this maneuver, I'm astounded. It's truly remarkable what a well-coordinated team can accomplish within such a brief timeframe.

As the team enters, clearing room after room, they apprehend anyone present. Smith and I listen intently over the radio, waiting for our cue to take action.

We remain in a supporting role. I, an FBI agent, and he, a local detective, understand the importance of entrusting specialized tasks to those most proficient in their roles.

The entry team leader's voice crackles through the radio, "Four in custody, five friendlies."

I exchange a glance with Smith. The call indicates that outside the perimeter, they have successfully detained four suspects, and more importantly, the girls are safe.

For the first time in hours, I feel my heart rate slow. The tactile team begins to bring out the suspects one by one, and Holt and I move in to assist the victims, now standing outside, witnessing the detainment of their abductors. The snitch was right. I count the girls, five in all. They're all underage, all in various stages of distress. Their clothes are tattered, faces dirty, hair unkempt.

When I enter the building, I am in disgust at what I see. These children were living in squalor on filthy mattresses in a large warehouse. There are cameras set up in various locations, which means they've been forced to be filmed. I feel sick to my stomach.

But I look at Smith because while that is awful, and while I'm sure as hell glad the SWAT team was able to enter and disband whatever was going on in this warehouse, it doesn't exactly help me with my goal.

Because sure, I'm looking for five underage girls, but I've been staring at their photographs for the last 24 hours. The thing is, these girls aren't the ones I'm looking for.

10 WILLOW

As I'm loading the dishwasher with my dirtied pans and plates from dinner, I think about the call with Linda. It's interesting how life presents us with reflections of our own experiences, giving us the opportunity to replay the past in order to grow from it. A sense of contentment washes over me, and even though I gave up spirituality for the most part after leaving the cult, there does seem to be a still small voice inside of me, reminding me that I'm growing, that I'm becoming a better version of me.

Maybe it's not the universe. Maybe it's just my intuition, as I learn to listen to my own gut. I feel content as I fill the dishwasher with detergent and press start on the load. Then I head over to the security system by the door and do my usual nighttime check.

I walk from room to room, closing down the house for the night, thinking about the clothing that I ordered with one-day shipping. I'll have some cute outfits to wear if Holt asks me out. And if not, I'll have cute outfits to wear when I take myself out. Maybe I should be doing that more, taking risks with my time, not always sitting in the cabin, attempting to live in a cocoon of my own making. Malcolm's asked me to go to trivia night again, and I suppose the cute tops I ordered could be a step up from the usual fleece I pull on over a t-shirt.

As I turn off the kitchen light, I hear a ping from my laptop alerting me to a new email. My laptop is sitting on my coffee table where I was doing my online shopping, and I walk over to it half expecting it will be a message from Holt. My lips twist as I realize it's not. I'm disappointed he didn't text me to let me know how his night turned out, but then again, he's working hard and the last thing he needs is someone expecting too much from him.

I'm surprised though to see the one-line email from my new student, Connor. *Hey Professor Willow, have you seen the news?*

It's a simple email, and I reply quickly. *No, I haven't had it on all night.*

He replies immediately. *It's scary how dangerous these things can be.*

I frown, reaching for my remote and turning on the television mounted above the fireplace, clicking through channels until I find the news. I close my laptop, not wanting to be distracted as I read the captions about five girls who were held against their will in a Seattle warehouse. I press my hand to my mouth as I realize this is where Holt was tonight.

There are SWAT teams, the Seattle Police Department, and the FBI all on this case. The footage is from a helicopter flying over the warehouse. I know it has to have been Holt, and I feel a little crappy for being disappointed he hadn't texted me.

I can't imagine the weight of his job.

I turn off the TV and head to my bedroom. My phone is charging on my bedside table and I reach for it, typing a text to him before I go to bed. *Hey,* I type. *I just saw the news. I'm here if you need to talk.*

I set my phone down and go to the bathroom to wash my face for the night. The warm water is refreshing, and the moisturizer rejuvenates my skin. I am glad I am taking the extra time to take care of myself. I put on flannel pajama bottoms and a black tank top. Pulling back my bedding and getting into bed. I feel warm and grateful, but also concerned about the wellbeing of the missing girls.

I pick up my phone one last time to see if he's replied, but there hasn't been a response. I lie down, trying to get comfortable, wanting sleep to come easily.

I toss and turn for about thirty minutes before I reach for my phone again. Still no message, but this time I pull up the meditation app I use regularly – the one I recommended to Linda -- and put on a sleep story. The soothing words as someone begins to describe the Amazon rainforest lulls me to sleep.

I don't know what the future will hold, but at least tonight, those girls won't be held hostage anymore.

11 TODD

I HAD PLANNED on leaving for a kayak trip for the past two weeks. God knows I needed it. With three teenagers in the house and a wife who is constantly on my ass, I needed a chance to breathe. Working from home was a good idea until I realized how chaotic my household actually is.

It's not that I don't love my kids or my wife. It's just very hard to get any alone time anymore. I think I underestimated how much I appreciated my commute back and forth to the office each day.

Now though, I'm in my kayak. A real beauty I got last year for Father's Day. As I think about it, pushing the oar through the water, I realize how big of a dick I sound. Hell, the kids picked this out for me. They wanted me to have a chance to get outside more often, and here I am complaining about how chaotic they are. I shake my head. When will I ever learn to be thankful for what I have?

I have a stable job that allows me to be home and see my kids grow up, that gives me the chance to unload the dishwasher or switch the laundry when my wife's volunteering at the kids' high school. I really am a piece of shit. Still, I am thankful for the moment and as I push the oar through the water, I take in a deep inhale and glance up at the sky. It's blue and brilliant. Something I know I'm going to miss as most of the winter will be a cloudy rain shower here in the Pacific Northwest.

But as they say, people have a hard time appreciating the good things they have because they take them for granted. I don't want to be like that. Not anymore.

When I get home tonight, I'm going to tell Jackie that she's got to take tomorrow, maybe even the whole week off. It feels like I'm having an epiphany and I've only been on the water for an hour.

As I move down the river, I watch a bald eagle soar above. I reach for the phone in my pocket vest and snap a quick picture, knowing Jackie will love it. It gives me an idea. Maybe I should take her bird watching this spring. We'd talked about it years ago when we were first married, just the two of us going somewhere quiet, maybe an island, Orcas or San Juan for a long weekend.

I realize I don't have cell service and can't send her that message right now, but decide I'll do it later. I want her to smile. I've probably been bringing far too many frowns on that woman's face over the years. I watch as another bird, a hawk, flies and lands on the rocky shore. My eyes follow it as I see it inching closer to a carcass.

At first, I assume it's a dead animal, but as I paddle the kayak closer to inspect the situation, my gut falls.

It's a human.

I navigate the kayak ashore, dragging it onto the rocks and stepping closer to inspect the situation. My jaw tightens and stomach clenches.

It's a young girl. And while I have three boys, it still hits way too close to home. A child dead, alone, in the November cold, dried blood on the rocks, her hair sprawled out around her. She's wearing a winter coat that's been ripped, and I wonder where she came from, how she got here. She's all alone with no pack, nothing. She's not even wearing proper shoes, just a pair of old Converse. What was she doing out here alone?

I pull out my phone again, but there's still no reception. Realizing I'm going to have to hike to higher ground to establish a cell signal, I drag my kayak even further up the beach so that it won't wash away. Once I move it off the shore, I hike to higher ground, to the cliff directly above the body. I press my lips together, surveying the situation. Could she have fallen from here? It would've been a clean fall and the highway is not too far to the right. Did she kill herself, or did someone do this to her?

I run a hand over the base of my neck feeling sick to my stomach as I call 911.

"Nine-one-one, what's your emergency?"

"I found a body. I'm down at the Hyacinth River, close to the parking lot. There's a girl...a girl on the shore. She's dead." I give the operator as much information as I can, but there's not much to say. The operator gets my story, before letting me know that someone is being sent in immediately.

My whole body is tense, this is not how I anticipated spending the day.

I send a quick text to Jackie. *I love you and the boys so much.* I press send, but not before adding the photo of the eagle to the message.

I walk back down the hill to where my kayak has been stored. I sit on the shore and look at this girl, who died all alone. If a wakeup call was what I needed, I got one.

I'm done taking anything for granted. My kids, my wife, my work. Life is too short. It can be taken from us in the blink of an eye.

I look up to the sky. The eagle still soars.

I swallow and say a prayer for the life I still have. For the life that this girl lost.

12 WILLOW

WE REACH THE TRAILHEAD, and I make a few closing remarks on today's lecture. I look at my students, underneath the crisp blue sky of this late autumn day, feeling so lucky to be here at all. We've been discussing the survival mechanisms that kick in once a person escapes a cult and the long-lasting effects it has on a survivor's life.

"Listen," I say to my students, "no matter how big the gap of time or distance a survivor puts between them and their past, the threat to safety remains so fragile and will keep them looking over their shoulders for the rest of their lives. Survival is about more than staying alive. It's about learning to become safe in a world that has shown you it's not a place that you can trust."

Caroline, one of my students, raises her hand. "Eventually, I guess the goal is for a survivor to learn to thrive instead of simply survive?"

I nod, giving her a smile. "Exactly," I say. "That's the ultimate goal. Of course, it isn't something that takes place overnight. It can take a lifetime to relearn and retrain your mind. Easy, simple things that maybe you or I could put into practice, like daily meditation, walks, yoga, or some sort of fitness and learning to create friendships or relationships with people in your new world, are all aspects that could be easy for someone who hasn't been in survival mode," I explain. "But someone who is just learning to rewire their brain and navigate a society that is free... it's a struggle. And that's why learning how we can help these people as psychologists and trainees is essential to being a part of the change we want to see in the world."

As class comes to an end and my students part ways, I think of Linda and the conversation from last night. She is trying to close that gap, getting a job that is going to give her a better life and more opportunity. And she's more than a survivor. She escaped that cult more than once, which means she's determined to make a different life for herself. There is hope.

As I wrap up my lesson and the students begin to disperse around campus, I see Dean Clarence walking toward me at the trailhead. I can read from his face that he must have listened to the end of my lecture. He's frowning as if he's already full of opinions. It bothers me to see his attitude, but I'm not going to let myself get derailed by a man who makes assumptions about me.

I notice Connor has held back a bit, even though the other students have left. He gives me a reassuring nod, and something about his look gives me a slight bit of comfort. I remember the email he sent me last night to check the news. It was actually sweet of him to even think of me and make sure I stayed up to date.

Dean Clarence walks closer.

I take a deep breath and plaster a smile. "How can I help you?" I say to him.

"I just wanted to come find you. I know you're always outside doing your classes, which, to each their own."

I withhold the urge to roll my eyes. "At Conifer College, I thought we are able to teach however we want. You know I always do my lectures outside."

"Sure," Clarence says, "but I wanted to talk to you, and you weren't in your office."

"Right," I say slowly. "Because I was teaching my class."

Clarence wore a look of exasperation. "I saw the article written about your involvement with the last FBI case with that girl, Jackson's daughter."

I nod. "Yeah. I didn't ask to have my photo taken. It just happened. I was outside Carter Jackson's building when we helped Amy get away from her entrapment.

Dean Clarence nods slowly. "Yeah, well, the president isn't exactly wanting to field these uncomfortable questions about your role here, within the department."

"My role here?" This time, I do roll my eyes. "Look, my involvement in that case was strictly to assist Agent Holt."

Clarence gives me a skeptical look, making a dismissive remark. "Your reasoning in helping the FBI may be more personal than professional."

"You know nothing about me, or my personal life, or what I'm doing with the FBI. They came to me twice, and it's bullshit for you to come here while I'm finishing a class and judge me. I can work with the FBI however I want. It's not doing anything to infringe on my contract with the college."

"I just thought you'd like to know that President Orsen isn't happy with your involvement. You're on thin ice."

I scoff. "Thin ice? Neither of you know anything about me, and I think we should keep it that way."

I walk past Dean Clarence, not wanting to walk on his heels back to my office.

Connor approaches me as I walk across campus, breathing deep and staying present with the scenery as I let the movement calm my nerves. I exhale, looking over at him. He's tall, maybe closer to thirty years old than I originally thought. He has dark brown hair and milk chocolate eyes. He closes the distance between us and nods at me.

"So how much of that did you hear?" I ask him.

"Enough to know that that the dean's got his head up his ass if he thinks anything you did shined a negative spotlight on the school." He adds, "Hell, I wouldn't be here now if not for you."

This makes me smile. I appreciate his support. "I wanted to thank you for that email last night. It was unexpected."

"Yeah," he says, starting to walk alongside me back towards my office. "I wasn't trying to overstep and get in your business. I just thought it was interesting, and that you might have insight on how one might help girls in situations like that. It's not a cult that they were a part of, but they had been kidnapped and held against their will. Kind of like Amy Carter."

I nod, taking in the information. "I can get you some notes from my lectures from before you joined the class. They might give you some insight, and also some book recommendations."

"That would be awesome," he says. "Hey, I was wondering though," –

he rubs a hand against the back of his neck, his expression turning sheepish – "if you got time for a cup of coffee?"

I twist my lips. We've just reached the building where my office is located, and I wonder if it's inappropriate and maybe out of line to get coffee with a student. "Maybe it's better to meet during office hours," I suggest, remembering Malcolm's TA, whose obsession got him canned a few weeks ago. I don't exactly want to be seen as a professor who skirts the line with my students. Perception is reality. And like Dean Clarence said, I'm already on thin ice.

Connor leans in making sure he's out of earshot of anyone passing us. His breath against my neck as he whispers in my ear has me slowing and pulling away. Not because I mind him being close, but because I wonder if he's looking for something more than a student-teacher relationship. That is something I am not game for.

"Listen," he says, "I'm a survivor too." At that, I step back. A strange rush of surprise runs through me. The momentary physical connection, coupled with the powerful information Connor just revealed, has me reassessing.

"How do you know I survived anything?" I ask him.

"After reading your books and lecture notes, I put it together. No one would have so much insight on what a survivor would be feeling unless they were one themselves. I wanted to transfer into your classes because I thought maybe you would understand me. That we could understand one another."

My eyes widen as I consider his words. He was able to read between the lines and see me for who I am, and why I do the work I do. "Well, I'm glad you joined my class," I tell him, "And honestly, I *would* like to talk to you more. Sorry for saying no right away to the coffee. It is just that you are a student and I want to keep things professional..."

My words trail off, suddenly feeling a connection with Connor I wasn't anticipating It would be nice to talk to someone who understands and knowing that it could only be platonic since he is a student of mine, makes me feel like this is a safe person to open up with.

Maybe he will get me in ways no one else has. "Look, I'd love to get coffee."

He grins. "Now?"

I nod. "That sounds perfect."

13 AGENT HOLT

I RUN my hands over my eyes, trying to wake up, only able to think of one thing: Coffee. That's what I need before anything else. Very strong coffee. I fell asleep at my desk at some point, in the middle of the night. Driving away from the crime scene last night was a major blow. I genuinely thought we were so close.

The sense of deflation and the loss-of-investigation energy can't be understated. We were all ramped up for the takedown only to find out we were wrong. But we did save very young girls from a disgusting situation. That counts for something.

I make a concerted effort to wake up and groan as I pull up my email, wanting to look at the case file from the beginning. It's going to need a total reworking of the case facts prior to the interruption.

Last night was painful. I'm glad those girls were released from captivity. What kind of monsters kidnap young girls and store them in a warehouse for sex trafficking?

Someone who should be locked up for life, or worse. I'm trying to get myself in investigative mode, but before I can focus on these files filling my computer screen, I've got to get some caffeine. I walk down the hall to the kitchenette and pour myself a cup of coffee. I'm drinking it black because I know from experience no amount of cream or sugar can make it taste any better.

I look around, wishing there was something on the community table to eat, but there's nothing but a box of stale donuts on the counter. My stomach grumbles, and I reach for an old-fashioned that's hard as a rock. I dunk it in my coffee and take a bite. The sugar mixed with the caffeination should give me the jolt I need to get myself back into investigative mode. As I walk back to my cubicle, I pass a few agents as they're trickling in for work.

Jedd, my buddy who works opposite me, claps me on the back. "Dude, I saw the news."

I shrug. "It wasn't the plan."

"Still, it's pretty awesome that you were able to get those girls out of that situation."

I nod, running a hand over my jaw, which is in desperate need of a shave. "Yeah, I'm glad the girls are getting back home. But there are five more girls I need to find."

As I sit down at my desk and chug the coffee, Lucinda, an analyst at the agency, comes over with a smile on her face and a folder in her hand.

"It's too early for that," I tell her, knowing she is always a chipper over-achiever.

"I was coming over to congratulate you." Lucinda grins at me. "I saw the news last night. Everybody has." She looks over at Jedd and they share a knowing nod.

I give a half-hearted smile. "Thanks, but I've got to get back to this case."

"That's why I came over. That's why I'm smiling." She wiggles her eyebrows and I'm not sure if she's trying to flirt with me or what, but I'm not feeling it. I've got my sights set on Willow, even if Willow doesn't have her sight set on me.

Still, Lucinda licks her lips, and pats the folder in her arm. "Look, I'm trying to do you a favor because you've been working so hard." She pulls up a chair and scooches it close to me, so close our hips touch.

I swallow, looking over at her. "All right." I say. "What do you got?"

"Well, look at this." She opens the folder. "It's a list of all the white vans within the Seattle area."

"How long did this take you?" I ask her.

Her eyes sparkle. "I pulled an all-nighter too."

I look her over and she sure as hell doesn't look like she was up all night. Her hair is perfectly curled. Her eyes are bright and her clothes aren't wrinkled. Considering my appearance at the moment, I look like shit. "Damn, Lucinda, thanks. This is a lot of work."

"I was able to use the different databases to build out this list. DMV records and other systems helped me gather intel. And since we have a better database to cross reference than the police department, I figured I was the one to do it. We've run the DMV records and cross-referenced them against the registered owners. And based on the percentage of abductors being male, I further culled the list."

Jedd whistles, "Damn, Lucinda, who's good side are you trying to get on?"

I shoot him a glance, both of us knowing Lucinda has always had a bit of a thing for me. I don't give him anything to fuel his fire.

"Okay," I say, "that's really great."

"I know, right?" She beams with a smile. "And once I had the names of male owners, I cross-checked them against a criminal offender database and highlighted any that had a history of sexual misconduct or violence. That said, I've trimmed the potential list down from over three-thousand vehicles to twenty-eight."

I nod, surprised. "Shit, that's amazing—"

"I know, twenty-eight is still a lot. It's a lot of people in vehicles to look into, especially considering the timelines that these girls went missing." Lucinda grimaces, adding, "that list of twenty-eight doesn't take into account the fact that the person responsible for the abductions may have no criminal record at all."

Jedd pipes in. "And if that's the case, it opens the search to a much wider range of potential suspects."

Lucinda nods. "Exactly. Sorry, Holt. I am trying to lighten your load as best as I can."

"No, this is incredible. This is really, really helpful."

"Hey, do you want another cup of coffee?" she asks as she stands.

I shake my head. "I'm good, but thanks." I don't want to give Lucinda any wrong ideas. I run my finger down the list once she's walked away, looking for that investigative tingle that might tell me where to start. I know it sounds weird, but it works sometimes. I stare at the list of potential subjects hoping I get a gut feeling on where to go.

Sometimes it works, sometimes it doesn't, but it's what separates a good agent from a great one, in my opinion. Though, I'm not going to tell anyone that because I know how cocky it sounds. And I don't have any reason to be cocky right now, considering my mojo is depleted, and I can't home in on any clue in particular.

With that said, I decide I need to take it from the top. I down the last drop of my coffee as I prepare to head out, but before I leave the agency, my phone rings. I answer it and find a sheriff's deputy on the other side of the line. "How can I help you?" I ask.

"I'm on the scene of a dead body found in the woods out by Hyacinth River."

I stop in my tracks. "What do you know?"

"Well, we've confirmed the identity of the girl."

A chill runs down my back. A girl, dead in the woods.

"We confirmed the identity and got a packet of information of all neighboring agencies with a list of the girls who went missing. I figured you'd want to be on the scene as we worked it. The girl who's dead is one of yours. It's Ruby Fallon." The deputy's words hit me in the gut, and I know I need to head out immediately. I grab a notepad on my desk to record all the information as he offers it. "Do you know the cause of death?"

The deputy tells me no. "It's hard to tell from the damage, but it looks like she may have fell."

"Fell?" I wasn't expecting that.

"Yeah, she was at the bottom of a cliff on the shore of the Hyacinth River."

I end the call and bolt out the door. As I do, I receive a text from Willow. I realize I'd never messaged her back last night after she asked how I was holding up – she'd seen the news too. She asks if we can reschedule our dinner for tonight.

I send her back a brief message. *Sorry, we'll have to see. I'm still working a case.*

I send Smith text a quick text, filling him in, before shoving my phone back in my pocket knowing I'm going to need to get another cup of coffee before I make it to the new crime scene.

14 CHELSEA

I'M AWAKENED by a rustling in the brush beside me. It's a squirrel. Fluffy-tailed and staring at me with beady black eyes. I blink, my eyes meeting his as I shiver uncontrollably. I've never thought to be jealous of a squirrel before, but the fur on his body is something I wish I had.

My body feels rigid and stiff from spending the cold night on a rock, losing the battle to maintain its natural heat. I wasn't able to make a fire, and now I'm so cold. I think of what my dad would say. He'd probably assess me, look at my nearly blue hands, and say I'm in a pre-hypothermic state.

My mind is a blurry fog. My stomach gnaws at me, having been empty for a couple of days, and coupled with the cold, I feel like things can't possibly get worse. My head throbs. I can't even cry. It's like my body knows I can't waste tears. I need to stay hydrated.

On my hands and knees, I look for dry brush and twigs, knowing I have to make a fire if I'm going to get myself through this day. My whole body trembles. My wrists are sore as I crouch low, reaching for sticks. Eventually I find a few that I can use to create enough friction to get the fire going. And gosh, I need to warm up so badly, my fingers and toes are numb and my strength feels nearly gone. I need to rest, but I'm scared to let my guard down.

Then I think of Dad. He must be so worried.

I can't give up. Not now, not ever.

I tear off more fabric from my already-torn jacket, using the cloth as I try to start a fire. I spin the sticks together with the shred of fabric, knowing Dad would be proud. I mean, he would also be terrified. Knowing him, he's probably scouring all the neighboring streets of Seattle looking for me. He's a fighter and also the one who taught me how to survive. That's why I'm still here breathing. Trying.

When I think of the night I escaped the van, it is easy to feel like an idiot. Maybe I should have never made the escape into the dark of night. Maybe I should have stayed crouched with those girls in the back of that cold van, praying for a miracle.

But I couldn't wait for a miracle to find me. I needed to be one all by myself.

If the other girls had followed me out, I wonder what would have happened to them. As I try to make the fire, I wonder where they are right now. By a stroke of luck, Ruby and I escaped. Well, I escaped. She's gone.

Those other three girls, they could be gone too.

My chin quivers at the thought. Are they in a better or worse state than I am? They might be somewhere warm, but I know the look in the eyes of those men who captured us. They were not the sort of men who would keep them warm on purpose. I think I'd rather be dead than be their prisoner. I know that's a pretty dire thing to say, but I feel like they had one purpose when they captured us. Their sole desire was evil.

As the fire before me begins to catch, I think that at least here, I'm free.

As the small fire grows, I begin to build it up. Needing to warm myself, I add the dry branches and twigs to the flame. I crouch as close as I can, trying to absorb all the heat, wanting the cold aches in my body to fade. I need to get warm enough to even stand on my own two feet and set out for a water source.

Even though I'm scared to return to the riverbank – even though I'm scared to go anywhere – I know I must. Of course, I don't want to get tracked by a coyote or a human -- a human predator, that is -- but I do want to find a road. I do want to find someone who can call for help, call my dad. I don't want to spend another night out in these woods. If I'm forced to, I'm scared I won't be able to make it to see another day.

I press my fingers to the back of my head, feeling the big lump that has formed and the gash where I struck the tree. The stinging pain against the light brush of my fingertips makes me wince. I spend another few minutes at the fire before I know I have to get to water to clean out the cut. My hands stay steady over the warm glow. I lean my face over the small flames, relishing in how it seems to defrost my nose, my cheeks. I look at my torn jacket, where I added to the rip so I could start the fire, and I tear a little more off, tying the red nylon to a visible tree branch. I know my father will come looking eventually, and if he does, this will help him find me. And all I want right now, is to be found.

15 WILLOW

CONNOR and I decide to head downtown to Olympia Coffee Roasters. We walk through campus, chatting about our mutual love of the little café. When we reach the parking lot, he walks in the other direction and waves goodbye. "That's me in the Volvo," he says, getting in an old beater car.

I smile, telling him I'll see him in a few, and get in my own vehicle.

As I turn on the ignition, I check my phone for any text messages. I'm not trying to overthink things, but before I left for work this morning, I'd texted Holt, checking to see if he wanted to reschedule dinner for tonight. But he never even replied to the message I'd sent last night about seeing him on the news. And the message I got this morning about dinner was a brief, *We'll see.*

Now, he has left a text telling me that he'd like to meet at Chez La Vin at seven tonight if that works.

It is still a brief message with no comment about his case, so I simply send him a one word reply: *Yes.*

I don't want to overanalyze his words – text is not the best form of communication, especially if you're trying to gather a tone – but his recent messages are much different than they've been in the past. It's not that I'm looking for sunshine and rainbows in every text thread, especially considering his line of work, but he did want to make plans with me. His hot and cold behavior is work-related – not about me.

I put my car in reverse and head downtown to the coffee shop. When I get there, Connor is waiting outside. We walk in together, and I breathe in the rich scent of the dark roasted beans. Comfort and warmth wrapped into one little shop. I love this place. It has a modern ambiance and a minimalist aesthetic.

I order myself a lavender latte, and Connor gets a caramel macchiato. He pays for both our drinks, which feels a little odd, considering I have the full-time job and steady income. At the same time, it seems even stranger to argue about who's paying. "I got it," he says, "honestly."

"Well, why don't I get us something to eat? Do you want a cookie or a muffin?"

We both land on lemon bars, and I pay in cash. A few minutes later, we're sitting at a corner table with our drinks and snacks. It feels comfortable, sitting here with Connor. He smiles warmly at me, and my shoulders fall, settling into the moment.

"So," he says, "I did want to thank you again for meeting me for coffee."

"It's good," I say, "I'm glad we could meet up."

"I know I'm your student and everything, so I'm not trying to be strange, but I am 29."

"Oh," I say, taking that information in. "I'm 35."

"Right. Well, I'm just saying ... I don't know what I'm saying," he says, chuckling, running a hand through his hair. He smiles at me, and our eyes lock.

I look away, taking a bite of the lemon bar, not wanting to cross any lines. Instead, I decide to focus on what the connection that brought us together is. I cut to the chase. "You're a survivor?"

He nods. "Yeah. I was in a cult in Southern Oregon," he tells me. "I grew up there. When I was younger, I always just thought we were like some hippy-dippy commune. I didn't know any better, because I didn't go to a school, and I didn't have any friends or a reason to leave the community. Every once in a while, we'd go into town for grocery shopping or whatnot, but we had a big farm, and we had a dairy. It was a pretty self-sufficient setup."

I nod. "How large was the group?"

"About fifty."

"The group's not that large then," I say. "What made it a cult, as opposed to a collective group of people in a shared housing environment?"

He nods and takes a sip of his coffee. "Well, that's a great question. I'd say the fact that I was forced to have sex when I was underage."

"Oh God. I'm so sorry, Connor."

He shrugs and doesn't look directly at me. "They had these rites... This whole messed up, creepy ceremony."

"How long ago did you leave?"

"Ten years ago. The whole organization was disbanded after a thirty year run. You can read about it, the Sanctity Settlement."

"Oh, I have read about that." I shake my head, trying to look into his averted gaze. "God, I'm so sorry, Connor." I have an urge to reach across the table, but I know that's not appropriate. Instead, our eyes meet again, and I feel as if I reach directly inside his heart instead.

I swallow, deciding to open up. "You were right about me. I was in a group myself. It was a polygamist cult on the Washington coast."

He frowns. "Are they still intact?"

I nod. "I think so, at least. I left when I was 21 and intentionally kept my distance. I've always kept a low profile because of that."

"Is that why you don't have a picture on your book biographies or anything?"

I gave a half-chuckle. "Yeah. You noticed?"

"I did. I even noticed that you don't have a picture on the school website."

"You did your research," I say with a bit of a laugh.

"I only noticed it when I was registering for classes. I was reading the different teacher bios and everything."

"That makes sense," I say. "But yeah, I changed my name and I started over."

"That must have been hard," he says.

"Well, I'm sure you can relate."

"Yeah. But I had the police. I had social services help me, since I'd only just turned nineteen. I wasn't on my own. If you escaped, then I'd guess you were fending for yourself."

I nod and take a sip of my coffee, allowing the memories of that time to come to the surface. "I was, but I somehow had a good head on my shoulders. I don't know if I'd manifested the right situations to come my way, but I met a lot of good people along the course of the year after I left. They helped me start again. I found someone who helped secure documents for me, who got me a Social Security card, all sorts of things that helped me start a new life."

He nods slowly, finishing his bite of the lemon bar. "Are you illegally teaching?"

"No," I say, only a little surprised by the question. "I had a birth certificate. That helped me get my things squared away so I could attend college, pay my taxes, stuff like that."

"Why didn't you go to the police about what happened to you, about the cult? Don't you want to take them down?" Connor asks.

I swallow, taking a moment to digest the question. "I still care about some of the women there. I don't want any harm to come their way."

"But aren't they *in* more harm," he asks, "by being taken advantage of?"

I look him in the eyes. "I understand why you might think that, but it's more complicated than that."

His words still hit home. They sting – more than sting. They pierce. I carry a shame with me still flaring inside my body as I sit there, trying to focus on the lavender latte, trying to keep the reminders of my past at bay. Reminded of the reason I'd left Fountain of Faith. And how fear has kept me from going to the police. While I'm not there anymore, so many other people are. People like Bethany.

I'm not strong enough to face all of my past. And as a professor of cult psychology and behavior, admitting that would mean losing my entire reputation.

The fact that I'm scared to face my past makes me feel weak. All I want is to feel strong. After years of feeling like nothing but a body to be used by a powerful man, the last thing I want right now is to lose my job, lose this life I've carved for myself.

"Look," I say, grounding myself in the present moment. I am here, drinking coffee with Connor. I am not in the past. "I am really sorry for everything you've been through."

"I'm sorry for the things you've been through, too," Connor tells me, his eyes meeting mine. "I love talking with you. You make me feel understood because I know we've both been through similarly hard things."

I swallow, feeling just as seen. "I feel like you understand me in ways most other people don't."

"That's probably true," he says, "but don't you work with a lot of other survivors?"

I nod and tilt my head, playing with the sleeve on my coffee cup. "Yeah, but it's usually over conference calls. It's not face-to-face like this. It's not ..." I press my lips together, thinking. "It's just different."

"All right," he says. "If you ever want to talk more, you know where to find me."

We leave the coffee shop, and I get back in my car. As I close my door, I realize how flustered I feel, in a way I wasn't expecting when I'd agreed to meet for coffee.

Connor could walk away from that encounter and judge me for the ways I've stayed quiet about my past. Judge me for the ways I chose not to use my voice when I could have. In my gut, I feel a sense of embarrassment, of shame for the way I've chosen to live my life, moving forward while other people were left behind.

But I'm scared. I am still so scared, because if I spoke up and the police didn't believe me, I know who *would* find me. I know what they would do to me.

I would be killed. Or sacrificed.

An alert on my phone pops up. I have a stupid burst of hope that it's Holt, but it's not. Instead, it's just a calendar notification reminding me that I have a haircut in thirty minutes across town. I exhale, remembering my makeover.

Maybe that will get my mind off the person I'm not, and instead help me move forward to the person I want to be.

16 AGENT HOLT

I'VE BEEN out to Hyacinth River before. I came here on a beautiful spring day and went kayaking. I wanted to become a real Pacific North Westerner and had a great time trying. The river was flowing steadily, the sun was shining, and the hyacinths were gorgeous in their blue and purple blooms.

Today though, it's early November. Gray clouds are heavy in the sky. No sunlight, just a sense of dreary dread. The crime scene is taped off and multiple units are involved. When I get there, I have to hike down the hill to get to the river, and I try to imagine how this child ended up on this rocky shore.

A kayaker found her and I'm grateful he was here when he was. If her body had been washed away, we might have lost clues we are able to gather now. The body was photographed and examined before I got here, and even though I know I'm the agent on this case, I admit to being glad I don't have to see the child's body out here alone in the cold when she should have been tucked into bed at home.

When I arrive, I walk over to talk with the deputy who called me earlier. His name is Rob, and he is a straight shooter. He walks me through the scene without pretense.

"There seem to be no other signs of trauma. No gunshot or knife wounds are evident," Rob tells me.

I nod, taking it in. "And what about on the cliff up there? Were there any clues?"

"Maybe. We haven't scouted the area thoroughly yet."

I look up at the rocky cliff above. "I'm gonna head up there now. Want to come with?"

He nods, and we hike up together. The ground is muddy, and there are a lot of loose rocks – easy to trip on. The fall would be catastrophic, if not deadly. The girl couldn't have taken that path to fall though. She wouldn't have landed in the same place. When we reach the top, we begin looking around. Immediately, I notice footprints in the woods. Larger than a tween girl's.

"So whoever was driving the white van must have pulled off on the side of the road or something and crossed through the woods to this clearing. Whoever kidnapped her may have been making a last-minute stop, because this isn't the trail from the parking lot," I say.

Rob nods, placing his hands on his hips. "Exactly. It looks like some broken branches too." He points ahead. We walk through the brush and see tire treads in the muddy turn-off.

"Wherever they were coming from, they were pulled to a stop. If this girl got out," I say, "maybe she made a run for it. Maybe she accidentally flung herself over the cliff."

The deputy runs a hand over his jaw. "It all points to looking like a fall, but she could have been pushed."

"It doesn't look like it was a serial killer at least."

"Was that a potential theory?"

I shrug. "I hadn't ruled anything out. Someone had a purpose with these girls. They were all taken the same afternoon. But I am guessing if one of them escaped the vehicle, the attackers weren't well enough armed. If one of them got free, there was a miscalculation."

The deputy nods. "Which means they were potentially taking the girls for purposes other than murder."

I think about the girls found in the warehouse last night, how they would be videotaped for sex tapes to be distributed on the internet. Sickos, men with incredibly disturbed minds, took those girls.

I wonder what kind of twisted psychopath came after these children. Whoever they are, it is well past time I found them and brought justice.

"There's no indication of anyone else out there?" I ask Rob, knowing he's been out on the crime scene longer than I have. "No reason to believe the other girls escaped at the same time?"

"It's hard to tell. The footprints get lost because the underbrush was so thick. They weren't walking through mud. They were walking on top of brush, shrubs and moss."

I nod and concede as we walk back down the cliff, hiking toward the shore to the crime scene. As I take it in, I realize there's not much else for me to do out here. There's no clue as to who the bad guys are and the fact that this child wasn't hurt by the force of someone else changes the way we proceed. Someone wanted these girls -- *wants* them – and while at least one of them somehow managed to escape, she didn't survive. The whole thing is brutal.

I check the time on my phone and realize there is no way I can make it to Olympia in time. Coming out to Hyacinth River is going to push back my timeline on meeting Willow for dinner. I wince and run a hand through my hair. Dammit. I really didn't want to let her down again.

I shove my phone back in my pocket and when I look up, Rob is calling for me.

"What is it?" I ask, jogging over.

"A few officers took a different route from the road through the woods to the cliff. They found two sets of footprints. Small ones."

I realize this case might finally be cracking open. "Another girl escaped."

17 FLINT

TAKING custody of the girls was never going to be simple. There are always too many opportunities for error when you get a new member in the vehicle. But they should have been at the compound by now. All of them. And now we're missing two.

Benjamin calls me. I pick up the phone and begin pacing my office. The space is sparse, an old building that has never been renovated, the window has a splintered crack in it that has never been replaced, the furniture is second-hand. And with each step I take, the floorboards creak. Everything feels off.

"This better be good." My voice is as harsh as it should be. His job was to bring back all of the girls. He dropped off three yesterday and he's supposed to be finding the other two now.

"It's gotten complicated," he tells me on the phone.

"What do you mean, complicated?" I press.

"I mean it's a crime scene. There's no way we could have gotten the girl's body. And we tried looking for the other one, but it's impossible. Derrick says we should call it."

"You haven't found her?" I ask.

"No," he says. "We were looking for hours, but then the cops came. They took the body away, and we were looking in the woods for the girl, but we keep losing her. And now we gotta go. The last thing we want is to get caught."

"I sure as hell hope you don't get caught. You parked the vehicle far enough away that they wouldn't find you, didn't you? " I ask, wondering just how dumb this man is.

"Of course. We're playing it cool. But it's getting dark."

I roll my eyes. "So what are you doing now?"

"Well, we still have to get the other one. And until we do that, I guess we're just going to cool it. Everything's in motion. All under wraps. No need to worry."

"And you're going to be able to deliver by tomorrow?"

"I think so. We want to honor you. We want to do good by you. We didn't mean to lose the girls. The kid was ruthless. You saw what she did to me. I was knocked out cold."

I know he's not exaggerating. When they showed up here with the three girls they still had in custody, he was in bad shape. Maria, our nurse, made sure he wasn't concussed and that they could get back on the road to recover the body of the dead girl, and try to locate the missing one. They've been gone for a day now and look at them. Two fools incapable of completing one mission.

"I gave you this task because I thought you were capable of seeing it through. The Lord asked me to give you this responsibility."

"I know," Benjamin says. "I don't want to disappoint you. I know that you're trusting us with so much."

"I am," I say. "And you've let me down, Benjamin. You and Derrick both. And so help me, God, if you fail me now – "

"We won't," Benjamin says. "I swear we won't. And next time you see me, I'll have that other girl with me. I promise. I'm going to find her."

"If you get caught by the cops, you realize we'll all be screwed, don't you? Don't do anything stupid, now. You understand?"

"I understand," Benjamin says. But I can hear him sniffling. I know he's crying. God damn it. Maybe I should have gone out myself, but that's impossible. My place is here with my fold, with the people who rely on me. They believe my prophecy and I can't give them any reason to believe it isn't coming to fruition.

Their job was to bring in these children for me. Five girls, for my family. That is the vision the Lord placed on my heart. I am not ready to let that dream die. Benjamin must hold onto his faith to see this through.

"I have faith in you," I tell Benjamin. "I have faith in you and Derrick."

"You do?" Benjamin croaks. "I'm so glad you said that. I thought I'd failed you. And..."

"Enough," I say. "No more crying, no more apologizing. Just finish the mission as it's been given to you."

"Yes, Father. Yes, Father Flint. May your will be done on earth as it is in heaven."

18 WILLOW

"So TELL me what kind of change you're looking for," Jenna, the stylist at the hair salon, asks me. I'm sitting in a chair with a cape draped around me, my hair parted and combed. She's running her hands through it and spreading it out with her fingertips, laying it over my shoulders, and inspecting.

"I just need a change," I say. "I'm open to anything at this point in my life."

Her face lights up in an excited grin. "I think we should do some layers around your face, really frame it to complement your jawline. I mean, maybe some fringe in the front. How do you feel about bangs?"

I press my lips together. "Bangs? I don't know. I've never had bangs before."

"Well if you're open to it, I think they'd really make your eyes pop."

"Pop?" I say, swallowing. I don't think anything about my appearance has ever *popped*. I'm intrigued. "Honestly? I trust you."

I look at her through the mirror. She's in her mid-twenties wearing trendy clothes. Her hair looks incredible, long and wavy, to the base of her back. Her makeup is flawless. She's literally glowing.

I smile. "I think I want what you have."

She chuckles, throwing her head back. "You want what I have? So you'd like some highlights too?"

"Is that what makes your hair bright?" I ask.

"Yeah. Have you been living under a rock or something?" She laughs. When I give her a blank look through the mirror, she softens and adds, "It's called balayage."

"Oh," I say, thinking it wasn't a rock exactly, but it was a cult for the first twenty-one years of my life. I've been playing catch up ever since. I wonder if that's how Connor feels now, like he is just trying to stay one step ahead, instead falling two steps behind.

"Okay, let's do the balayage then." She tells me the price, and I pull in a breath of surprise.

"Wow," I say. "I didn't realize getting a cut and color was so expensive."

"Balayage is great, though, because it will grow out without looking bad. I promise. And you can come back in six months to freshen it up."

"All right," I say flashing her a smile. "I suppose I'm worth it."

She rests a gentle hand on my shoulder. "Oh, you're definitely worth it. Now, let me get set up." She leaves to the back, and a few minutes later, she returns with a brush and a bowl of paint for my hair. She dips the brush into the paint and begins going to work. "So any reason for the big makeover?"

"I have a date tonight," I tell her.

"Ooh, that's fun. Where are you going?"

"La Chez Vin."

"That place is awesome. I went there once with my girlfriend when she got a promotion. The wine list is amazing, and I'm not even a wine person. But the cocktail list is amazing, too. They had this old fashioned that was made with mezcal. I don't even know what kind, but it was incredible."

"Okay," I say with a smile. "I'll make sure to try it out tonight."

"And I had this Bolognese pasta that was just melt-in-your-mouth delicious. They make all the noodles there, in-house."

I smile as Jenna continues talking on and on, going to town with my hair. The whole salon is abuzz, and I wonder how she does this job every day without her mind becoming mush. There are probably thirty different women in here in various states of haircut and color, stylists snipping with scissors and painting hair, laughing and telling stories, and I realize maybe that's what I've been missing. Girlfriends. I don't actually think I've ever had a real girlfriend. Not since Bethany.

"What's wrong?" Jenna asks, looking at me through the mirror. "You okay? I feel like I lost you."

I shake my head. "No, no. I'm good. I'm just thinking."

She relaxes and keeps working. "Do you do that a lot, get lost in your thoughts?"

"Maybe," I say. "I haven't really thought of it that way, but I'm a writer and so I guess it means I have a lot of time to think things through."

"Well that's interesting. Are you a full-time writer?"

I shake my head, although not vigorously. "I'm also a professor at Conifer College."

"Very cool. What do you teach?"

"Psychology, specifically cult behavior and conditioning."

Jenna pauses to lock eyes with me in the mirror. "Okay, that is *so* cool. Did you hear about the Harmony situation in Olympia a few months ago? I was obsessed with reading about it. I'm not usually a news person, but it's so close to home. And it's just crazy, those poor kids."

I swallow, reminding myself to take deep breaths in and out. I'm not going to get triggered by Jenna's words. I know she is just talking without realizing the impact. It's not personal. I don't want to tell her details, though, so instead I skirt the truth.

"I did read about it," I say. "I guess we never really know what's going on in our own backyard, do we?"

"Exactly," Jenna says. "My boyfriend? His house is haunted. Someone must've been murdered there at some point. So that's not even his back-yard. That's literally in the house."

I give her a smile, not thinking it's funny, but understanding what she's trying to say. "I don't know if a ghost means someone had to have been murdered. Maybe someone just died in one of the bedrooms," I say, doing my best to stay lighthearted.

"Okay, that's a fair point," Jenna concedes. "I don't know why I imme-diately went to murder. I think it's because I watch way too many true crime documentaries. And podcasts? Oh my gosh. I'm going to need to cut myself off because, like, why am I so fascinated with the way people are brutally murdered? It's kind of creepy, right?"

I nod. People are fascinated in general with worst-case scenarios. It's why the news cycle always tells us about those horror stories. It feeds our morbid curiosity and our desire to think our lives are better than they might really be.

A few hours and subject changes later, Jenna's finished my cut and color, and I must say I look better than I ever have. "What do you think?" she asks.

I turn my head from side to side, in awe of my flattering new appearance. "I think I look a few years younger. You covered up the gray."

"You hardly had any gray, but yes, it looks fantastic. So what are you going to wear to dinner?" she asks, removing my cape and handing me my purse and jacket.

"I was just going to wear this."

She laughs, then stops when she realizes I'm serious. "You can't wear that to La Chez Vin."

"I can't?" I ask her. "Well, I ordered some clothes online last night, but they're not here yet."

"You have to go to the boutique next door called Right Now. They have amazing customer service. If you walk in there and say you need something to wear to La Chez Vin, they'll pull a bunch of stuff off the racks and help dress you."

"Really?" I say. "I've never done that sort of thing."

She laughs. "Okay, you really have been living under a rock."

I take her advice, though, and head next door. An hour later, I am at a register with three new outfits for dates I may or may go on. However, none of it will be returned. I went into the changing room to make sure everything was my size. Whereas the online shopping I did last night may have been a disaster, considering I'm a size bigger than I thought I was in jeans, and I learned that button-downs don't exactly say sex appeal.

"These will look fantastic," the woman at the register says. She'd helped me find the right sizes and fits in all types of clothing. She hands me my bag, and I walk out of the store actually feeling more confident than I have in years. Maybe I need to get out more, spend some time around women. The ones I met today were friendly and helpful and kind. And even though the hair salon was much louder than the trails on Conifer College where I spend most of my time, and definitely louder than my cabin tucked away in the woods, there was something soothing about being around so many women.

In some ways, it reminded me of when I lived at Fountain of Faith. While we weren't allowed to wear makeup or do our hair, we were living communally. Women working on meals in the kitchen and taking care of children. Cleaning the kitchens and bathrooms, teaching kids to read and write, all done together with other women at our side.

But after I left, well after I'd escaped, I let that part of my life die because it was too painful, too hard to imagine being that close to a woman again and opening myself up.

But as I get in my car, stowing my shopping bag in the backseat, I think about Bethany again. Knowing when I left FoF, I'd left her behind too. She is someone I want to protect, but I'm scared her husband would hurt her if I told the authorities about what was happening there. I would never forgive myself if something happened to her. So I've kept quiet. But as I drive back home, I wonder if maybe being quiet hasn't protected anybody at all.

Maybe all I've been doing all this time is a pitiful job of protecting myself.

19 AGENT HOLT

THE TWO SMALL sets of footprints near the cliff lead us to believe that two young girls were out here. One was found dead at the bottom of that cliff on the shore of the river. The other though, we're not sure what happened, but it doesn't look like she turned around. She must have moved forward. I look at Rob and say, "She could have made the fall in the water. She could have gotten lucky."

"Hypothetically," Rob says, "say the van pulled over at the side of the road in that turnoff. Somehow these two girls escaped. Hell, maybe all of them did, but say these two did and they ran and got to a dead end, maybe they were being chased."

"That means the other girl might be out there," I say, finishing his thought.

"Somewhere on the river." Rob rubs his chin, his brows furrowed.

Everyone working the case begins to move quickly. If there's a search party that needs to get underway, we need to begin now before the coming darkness. Everyone working the crime scene moves into action, understanding the stakes. A girl, lost in these woods, for days. A child's life is in the balance.

As we begin walking down the river, my heart pounds with each step I take. The idea of finding her drowned would give me a sense of failure. I can't lose two out of five of these girls. Not when so many parents are counting on their children being returned.

I've got to find her breathing, living. I have no other choice.

We track along the river. It's shallow in some places and eventually, I see something up the riverbank about two miles downstream. "Look," I say, pointing ahead. I'm with two guys who work for the Sheriff's department, Antonio and Mark. "Do you see that?"

As a trio, we walk from the riverbank to a tree. "Someone made a fire, and not that long ago. Not today," I say. "At least, I don't think so."

"It could have been anybody," Antonio says. "Could have been a hiker. Someone out kayaking for a day trip. Even the guy who found the body of victim one."

"Possibly," I say, "but if you were a backpacker, you wouldn't have been using sticks like this. You would've come prepared. Someone desperate had to have made this," I say, looking at the sad remains of a fire.

I scour the ground. "Look, footprints." I point to the small footprints on the muddy riverbank. I look across the river, wondering if she would've crossed the stream. "What do you think?" I ask, wanting to loop the officers into my thought process. "I think she would've crossed here."

"Yeah," Antonio says. "Especially if she was scared, if someone was tracking her."

"And look," Mark says, "another set of footprints, the same size coming back down toward the river."

We decide to cross it. And in the distance, Rob sees me make the move. I give him a wave and call him on the radio. "We're crossing here. Have one of your guys collect the evidence left here. Looks like she may have made a fire."

I think about the temperature. It's been in the thirties. This poor girl would've been frozen half to death. Pre-hypothermic. As we walk across the river, our pants get soaking wet, our shoes drenched.

At this moment, I realize who it must have been who escaped.

Chelsea. Her dad Leroy is an Army Ranger. When I interviewed him, he told me how his girl was smart. *One smart cookie,* I think is what he said exactly. He mentioned that he'd been going hiking and backpacking with her for years. That she knew her way around the woods, that he was confident she could get herself out of anything.

The confidence her father has in her is impressive. And at the time, I didn't want to dishearten him by saying survival skills might not be necessary, depending on who had abducted his child, and why. But if she was out here all alone, maybe the skills her father had taught her are the ones saving her very life.

We hike down the other side of the river and a few miles in, we see several broken branches. We scale down a hill where vines and brush have clearly been recently trampled. "She might have fallen," I say.

Mark nods. "I think you're right. She must have been grabbing some of these branches and – "

"Shit!" I say. "Look." On one of the branches, there is a shred of clothing, maybe a jacket, red nylon. "We need to know what she was wearing when she was taken," I say, trying to remember the details Leroy gave me during our interview.

Rodriguez radios it to the deputy.

Daylight has given way to the growing darkness, and we're five miles from the crime scene. "We can't stop now," I say. "Now is the time. We've got to find her. Before we lose her forever."

20 WILLOW

As I sit at La Chez Vin, I feel wildly confident.

It's not that I usually feel insecure. I'm successful at my job, and I've made a great life for myself. But feeling this confident in the way I look is not a familiar feeling. My hair looks incredible. I'm wearing a new black dress and heels, which may be out of my comfort zone, but make me feel incredible. As I finish the first glass of wine and order a second, I realize it's been a long time since I'd felt so good in my own skin. It's been a lifetime.

When the waiter brings my second glass of wine and asks if the other person at my party will be joining me, I do begin to feel a bit of a letdown. "I'm not ready to give up," I tell the waiter, checking my phone again.

Holt is the one who'd made reservations at this place, but I haven't heard from him since the message earlier today when he confirmed the date, time, and place. Not wanting to assume the worst, I turn my phone over and take a sip of the wine. "He'll be here," I tell a waiter, "I think so at least. He has a busy job."

I swallow my words as the waiter smiles and walks away. While Holt does have a busy job, he also still has a phone. He still has the ability to contact me, or at least let me know if he wasn't going to show for the second date in a row. Right? He wouldn't do that.

Would he?

I look around the restaurant and realize that at the bar there is someone I know. Of all people, it's Connor.

When I realize we're both sitting alone, I stand and walk over to him. "Hey," I say, resting a hand on his shoulder. "So random seeing you here."

He sets down his book and his eyes brighten. "Professor Grace?" He's drinking a cocktail and I remember Jenna at the hair salon telling me their cocktail menu was great. I hadn't even remembered that when I sat down and ordered a glass of Cabernet.

"What are you drinking?" I ask him.

"An Old Fashioned," he tells me. "I heard they make some of the best in town."

"I heard that too, the mezcal one?" He nods and I ask, "Do you hang out at this bar often?"

He shrugs. "It's a bit upscale, but the bar is chill. I'm not really into the college scene. I prefer the quiet vibe of this place. I had a steak here last weekend and decided to come back."

"Are you having dinner here tonight?" I ask him. Holt is forty-five minutes late. I think I'm going to call it.

"I haven't ordered yet," he says. "I just got here a few minutes ago."

"No pressure," I say, "but my date didn't show and if you want to have dinner at my table, I wouldn't say no. I'm starving and am going to order for myself."

He chuckles. "Really? I mean, if it's not weird. I'm not trying to take your date's place or anything."

"No, I know that" I tell him. "At this point, I'm just hungry. I need to eat dinner and if he's not going to show, that doesn't mean I shouldn't enjoy a good meal."

"I like your attitude," Connor says, standing with his drink in hand. He turns to the bartender, "Can you add this to my tab? I'm going to sit at the table with her."

"Of course." The bartender smiles at us while he polishes glasses.

Connor and I walk into the dining room and take our places at the table that I thought would be for me and Paxton Holt. Even though it's potentially rude, I check my phone one last time. Still no message. I exhale, deciding to let it go.

If Holt doesn't want to have dinner with me, that's fine. The universe is opening new doors for me everywhere I seem to be turning, and today that's in the form of Connor.

"So," I say, "it's kind of funny, two encounters in one day."

He smiles. "You're right. It feels like coffee was forever ago. You look really different from when I saw you last."

I tuck my hair behind my ears. " I got my hair done. And put on a dress."

"Well, you look incredible," he says.

I feel my cheeks flush and wonder if it's from the wine or the compliments. Either way, Connor cleaned up nice too. He's in a collared shirt and dark denim jeans.

I clear my throat. "You mentioned steak, are you wanting that again tonight?"

He reaches for a menu and scans it. "I think I'm going to go with a shrimp pasta."

"That sounds good." I smile, now scanning my own menu.

Connor is easygoing and warm, which I appreciate about him. I have put so much hope on Holt. But maybe it wasn't so much the connection or chemistry I have with him as just learning to open myself up.

"I'm going to have the chicken piccata," I say.

"Sounds good."

The waiter comes around and we place our order, then pick up where we left off at coffee earlier, both of us diving deeper into our pasts. I sip my wine and tell him how I went to the University of Washington.

"It's amazing that you pulled up your bootstraps all on your own."

"I'm glad you see it that way," I say. "After we got coffee, I was wondering if you were judging me for the way I'd left without shining a light on where I grew up."

"It's not my place to judge," Connor tells me.

We engage in lighter small talk before our food comes rather quickly. We eat while he tells me about some of his other courses at the college. He seems engaged and really enjoying what he's learning. I finish my second glass of wine and order a third, grateful I rode here in an Uber.

We're laughing over one of his anecdotes about Professor Blador, one of my closest friends. Thinking about him, I realize I should probably make some space for that friendship too. I haven't seen him in the last few weeks and after everything he's done for me, I kind of owe it to him to put some time into the friendship, even if he was looking for a deeper connection than I was interested in.

"So," Connor says, leaning in. "I want to know what you're working on now. Are you writing a new book?"

"I'm working on something," I say, "but it's a little more personal than my other projects."

Intrigue etching his features, he asks what I mean. Maybe it's the wine, maybe it's the day, maybe it's the fact I feel so incredible with my new hairstyle and dress, but I'm in the mood to be uncharacteristically spontaneous.

"Well, if you want to drive me home, I could show you my office and let you see what I'm working on."

Connor smiles. "I would love nothing more."

21 AGENT HOLT

WE FIND A SECOND CAMPSITE. Chelsea is resourceful. I've braced myself for whatever we might find next, but the fact that she made it to night two and was able to make another fire, gives me some hope.

I begin to feel less hopeful though, when I see the smear of blood against a tree trunk she must have slept against last night.

"Head wound," I say.

Antonio nods.

"That's not good," Mark says, shaking his head.

The idea of this young girl alone out here is difficult for any of us to think about. No one wants to imagine that or what may have happened to her next. She may have made this fire, but that fall down the hill where the brambles and branches were broken means she hit herself hard at some point. Now she's bleeding from a head wound without any medical attention.

The temperature keeps dropping, and though the sky has given us the gift of no rain, it's growing colder than it's been all year. We keep following the tracks and see two more places where she's left pieces of her coat. She has intentionally tied the fabric to tree branches. It was like she'd left silent prayers through the woods, asking for help.

This was a risk she took since her captors could have been the ones tracking her. But the fact that she was willing to take that risk shows me she knows how much trouble she's really in, hoping against hope that it would be someone safe, who would find her.

And even though I'm not a thirteen-year-old girl, I know she must be scared. But even in fear, she is being smart. I remember how fondly her dad spoke of her. Maybe she was leaving these markings for him to find. I wish he was out with us now. His skills as an Army Ranger would come in handy.

But of course, we didn't know what body we would've found at the bottom of that cliff, and we didn't know what other girl may have escaped, so we didn't notify the parents at all. Not until we know something more concrete. Not until we find Chelsea.

We continue to follow the tracks, and just when I wonder if we will even find her – I see a child beneath a big pine tree.

I call out to Antonio and Mark. "She's here. Chelsea?" I call. "Chelsea." I shout. She lifts her head ever so slightly as I approach, she's shaking. Her eyes fall closed, and I run to her. She doesn't move at all. Her hair is matted. I shine a flashlight at her scalp and see blood. Dark red and dried. "Chelsea, I'm Agent Holt. I'm with the FBI. You're safe. You're safe now."

She doesn't register my words. She's in a hypothermic state and clearly the concussion has made her woozy. The head wound is deep. I radio to Rob. "We need medical transport immediately. A helicopter."

Antonio and Mark begin radioing others from the search party. The scene doubles within minutes as everyone moves to our location. Everyone on the lookout rushes toward us.

I crouch down with Chelsea, letting her fall against my chest as I wrap my arms around her. She's shaking. Ice-cold. She must be dehydrated and so hungry. A helicopter won't take long to get here now. We're so deep in the woods, there's no way we could carry her out ourselves.

I feel a sense of pride, holding her against me as a helicopter flies overhead, lowering toward us as it earmarks where we are from the flares Mark and Antonio set off. Everything has happened at warp speed, but I'm only focused on the child shaking against me.

Two girls have been found, one dead, and three more are missing. We won't know the manner of Ruby's death until the autopsy. Hopefully after Chelsea has received medical attention she can help with crucial information on the captors.

The helicopter hovers overhead, and a ladder is dropped along with a basket for the stretcher. A team emerges from the helicopter, moving quickly down the ladder toward us.

Chelsea's body is lifted and she is moved to the stretcher, where she is wrapped in thermal blankets. She doesn't even have the energy to cry. To ask what's happening. Her eyes are closed and she's lost. I pray she keeps conscious. I pray she makes it out alive.

People give cops a bad rap, talk shit about how much they pay in taxes for salaries, but it's moments like these that I feel a sense of pride surge through me for the people who give their lives to save others, to keep them safe. The team approaching us are heroes in their own right. And I feel honored to be here at all, to be part of the change I wish to see in the world because someone's got to step up. And everyone here, the men and women alongside me who've been searching for hours for this girl, the team at the hospital who'll be helping ensure Chelsea gets the care she needs, all of us working together for a common good.

It gives me a sense of pride that is hard to find in this world where pain and suffering overwhelms so many of our daily thoughts and choices.

There are no additional leads to the whereabouts of the other girls at the moment. It's late and we're going to have to resume in the morning. I watch the helicopter pull Chelsea up and away.

I shake my head. "Hell of a day."

A unit has been dispatched to meet us here in the woods. Apparently, Chelsea would've only had to walk a quarter of a mile uphill to get to a road. But she was lost and unable to navigate this terrain. If only she'd known how close she was to civilization, she might not have gotten to the state she was in.

We ride in cruisers back to the main parking lot. Before I leave to get in my car, I thank Rob for everything he did.

"It's you who found her," he says.

"You'll resume in the morning?"

He nods. "Yes, the search party will be out at the break of dawn."

I shake his hand. "Hopefully we'll find the other girls in one piece. That's what matters. More than anything."

He gives a tightlipped smile and we part ways after sharing goodbyes. When I get in my car, I think about the day I've had, and how all I want to do is tell Willow about it. While I could head home, what I really want is to see her face. And not just because I owe her an apology. That's part of it. I missed dinner again and I sure as hell hope she'll understand.

But more than apologies, what I really want is to give her a hug. Because after a day like this, I feel really alone.

22 WILLOW

CONNOR WATCHES me as I reset the alarm system. The cabin is quiet and dark. There's only one lamp on a side table casting a soft glow about the room. I know I had too much wine – more wine than I ever drink – and my guard is down. But I also feel light, like maybe this is how the evening needed to go after such a disappointment with Holt. For two dates in a row, he'd failed to show up, and this one, I didn't even get a text telling me he wouldn't come. I sat at that restaurant for forty-five minutes waiting for a man who never even showed.

I try to shake those thoughts away and focus on the present moment. Connor and I are just getting to know one another and already I feel like we understand each other at a deeper level than I have with most people. As I walk with him to the kitchen, I reach for two glasses thinking we both should have some water. He takes one from me after I fill it and drinks its entirety before setting the glass down on the counter. He points to the bottle of wine I had bought for my first-planned dinner with Holt.

"Shall we?" he asks, reaching for it. It's a twist top, and he's already opening it.

I laugh. "I don't know if I need another glass of wine, but I suppose it's not the worst idea."

I grab two wine glasses and Connor fills them. He takes the bottle and we each reach for our glasses before walking into the living room. We sit and he sets the bottle on the coffee table. He raises his glass and we clink the rims. "To surviving."

I shake my head. "No, Connor, we can't cheer to that." I smile. "To thriving."

He grins. "Now we're talking."

"You know," I say, "you are a student ..." My words trail off.

"I know," he says. "Should I go? Is this just too much?"

"No," I say cautiously. "It's, I don't know what it is. You are my student, but you're also older than my other students. And... I feel connected to you, like we understand each other."

"I feel that way too," he says, his mouth quirked up in a smile and his eyes glinting. "So where is this office you spoke about?"

I sip my wine and hesitate for a moment, but then I stand and walk to my office. I unlock the padlock and pull open the door. He stands and walks over to join me carrying his glass.

"So this is where the magic happens," he asks, "where you write all your books?"

"Pretty much," I say, flicking on a light.

"Can I ask why you lock it up? I mean, your house is already so secure."

I exhale. "It's all a facade, that padlock. It makes me feel better even though I know anyone could easily break through it. You need a bolt cutter or something and it would be done, but it's not about that so much as just feeling like I need another layer of protection. After everything I've been through, it's really hard for me to open up."

Connor looks at me, his eyes soft. "It feels like you're pretty good at opening up to me."

"Surprising, isn't it?"

He shrugs. "I don't know. Maybe it's a trauma bond."

"We didn't go through the same trauma though."

He laughs. "I know, just in general."

He looks around the office, stepping away from me. His eyes scanning over the cork board and my bookshelves. "You have quite a library in here."

I nod. "Yeah. I love reading and researching and ..."

"You're really special," he says, turning to me.

I swallow. "Well, thank you. You're really special too. And we're lucky. We got out of hard situations and look at us now." I smile softly.

"Look at us," he says, eyes still twinkling.

I try to control my quickening pulse, taking another sip of wine. "So how much longer do you have at school?"

"A couple of years, but I don't know. Maybe it's not for me after all."

"What do you mean?" I ask. "I thought you were enjoying the program."

"I like your class," he says with a laugh, "but I don't know."

"What do you want to do?"

"Make a difference," he says. "Make an impact. And maybe getting a college degree isn't exactly going to lead me down the path that I want."

"What kind of difference though?" I ask. "There are lots of ways you can make an impact in life."

"I know," he says. "That's what I'm still trying to figure out."

Just then, I see headlights through my living room window. I frown, looking out the door of the office. My alarm system beeps, alerting me that a car is here.

I frown. Who could be here this time of night?

Connor looks over at me. "Were you expecting company?"

I shake my head. "No, I wasn't." I walk out of the office and Connor follows me. I set my glass of wine down on the side table and pull up the camera on the tablet of the security system.

"Do you know who it is?" he asks.

As I look at the car. I exhale, realizing this is going to be awkward.

23 AGENT HOLT

By the time I get to Willow's property, I'm beat, and I know driving out here is a risk, but I just want to see Willow's face. It's pitch dark out and her driveway is long, but at the end of it there are two cars. Hers and someone else's. I'm instantly curious who she has over tonight.

I wonder if it's Malcolm sliding himself into position now that I'm gone. Maybe she called him over, frustrated with the way I didn't follow through two times in a row, but I don't think so. My impression from what she'd said is that Malcolm is interested in her in ways she's not reciprocating, and I don't think Willow's the kind of woman who would lead someone on. Maybe she's in one of her private therapy sessions, but that wouldn't make sense either, considering she usually does those remotely and she wouldn't have had one scheduled the same time as our dinner date.

I park my car behind hers and turn off the ignition. I walk to the front door and knock on it, sure Willow already knows I'm here. Her security system is state of the art and would've alerted her of a car pulling into her driveway.

There's no answer at first, and my mind immediately runs to the worst-case scenario, thinking maybe someone has found her – someone from her past. Someone she's been running from. Maybe someone's here to hurt her.

I pull at my gun on my hip as I hear voices.

Then there is the sound of shattering glass.

"Willow?" I call out, my heart racing.

A beat passes, then she pulls open the front door. Glass is shattered on the floor. I look into her widened eyes.

Willow sees my gun. So does the man standing behind her. I've pulled it out without hesitation. It was the sound of the glass breaking, the pause before she opened the door that worried me, that made me assume there was a threat.

"Holt," she says, looking at my gun.

The man behind her holds up his hands as if in defense. "Whoa, easy," he says.

I shoved my gun back in the holster. "Sorry," I say. "I heard the glass. You didn't answer right away. I was worried."

"I was just telling Connor who was here. I didn't want him to ... Well, I don't know. I'm just surprised to see you."

I swallow, looking the man over.

"This is Connor," she says in a more formal greeting, and my quick assessment of the other man gives me a pang of worry. He's younger, well-built, and extremely good-looking. He's dressed in a collared shirt, and I'm immediately struck with a deep sense of jealousy. It's something I've never really experienced before. The feeling leaves me unsteady.

Willow, though, tells me to step inside. "Just a sec," she says, "I'm going to get something to clean this up."

Connor clears his throat. "Let me, Willow. It's my fault. I'm the one who dropped the glass."

"No, really, it's fine," she says. She looks at me and then her eyes dart back to Connor before she makes her exit to the kitchen.

I'm standing there awkwardly, the front door still open, feeling like an idiot for pulling out my gun. What the hell did I think was going on in here?

But actually, what the hell *is* going on in here?

Willow returns with paper towels, a dustpan, and small brush. She cleans it up quickly.

"I think I got all the glass," she says.

Connor kneels down, finding an extra shard. "Luckily the glass was empty."

"Thanks," she says. Their fingers brush, and I feel like I'm standing in the way.

"I'm Agent Holt – uh, Paxton Holt," I tell him as Willow walks back to the kitchen to dispense of the broken glass.

"Connor is a new student," Willow calls out to me. This does little to soften the blow, though. In fact, it feels worse. The man standing before me looks too old to be one of her students. Maybe he's a graduate or in a Ph.D. program, which only worsens my sense of failure.

She must be enamored by this guy, which leaves me feeling inadequate. I ditched her for our date and he immediately swept in. I can't help but grimace. Smart guy.

With my weapon holstered, I stumble for words, knowing I look like a mess. My clothes are filthy from the search. My pants still wet. I feel beat.

Willow returns from the kitchen and, on the other hand, she looks better than I've ever seen her. She's in a black dress, and her hair looks different. Lighter and framing her face, making her eyes go wide, compounding my feelings of stupidity.

"I'm really sorry for interrupting. I did not realize you were having company." I stood there in silence for a moment longer before saying, "I should go."

Connor gives me a smug look that Willow doesn't notice, but I certainly do. I subconsciously squint my eyes back at him and begin to back out, but Willow pushes past Connor to follow me.

"Stop. Holt, stop. I didn't tell you to go. You can stay." She's close to me now and I want to wrap my arms around her. I want a hug. I know that's not fair to ask. She's not my person, not my girlfriend, but I can smell her vanilla perfume, something she's never worn before, and she looks earnestly into my eyes pleading with me to stay.

"Connor is really interesting," she tells me. "He has a fascinating life story and we were just sharing some things about our past. He was at the restaurant bar." She frowns. "The restaurant that I went to and sat alone for forty-five minutes." The pang of guilt in my chest is unbearable. Willow exhales. "Connor was there having a drink and anyways, I don't know why I am explaining all of this. Does any of that make sense?"

Connor appears in the doorway and walks down her front porch, sipping a new glass of wine as he watches our conversation.

"Look, Willow," I say focused on her, not him. "I'm sorry I didn't text you earlier. I was out in Hyacinth River all day, no cell service. The case I've been working on got really complicated. I'm so sorry, I totally let you down, and I'm embarrassed. If I could have done anything to change it, I would've, but --"

"Holt, it's okay," Willow says, then she pauses, looking me over. "But are you okay?"

"I'm fine," I say, knowing it's not the time or place to talk about it. Especially with Connor hovering behind us.

Willow frowns. "All right, well, will you call me? Maybe we can meet later this week?"

"Sure, of course," I say.

She reaches for my hand and squeezes it, but by then Connor is at her side.

"Well, it was certainly nice to meet you," he says smugly.

I swallow, stepping away. I get in my car feeling like an idiot.

Not sure what I was expecting, but that was not how I thought it was going to go.

24 FLINT

The compound has a sense of calm, peace.

But maybe that is wishful thinking.

The women and children are in their homes doing their daily tasks, the men of the fold are out working.

And I am trying to fix a situation that is getting out of hand.

It shouldn't be so complicated. After all, we're doing the Lord's work. I felt personally called upon to have these men follow out my plan. But it's becoming more obvious that no one is prepared to do this work except for me. I'm trying to be patient. But it's proving difficult.

"There's just been a slight complication," he tells me.

"I know that," I say. "I've been worrying about it for hours. The girl, Chelsea, was found in the woods this afternoon."

"Is she talking?" he asks me.

"As far as I know, she's still under evaluation at the hospital and it doesn't appear she's given anything to law enforcement. We need to ensure that doesn't happen. If necessary, I need someone to go into the hospital and take care of her. I'm not going to lose what we've built because a thirteen-year-old girl can't keep her mouth shut."

"But I thought she was one of the chosen," he asks me. "One that was to be brought into the fold."

"Are you questioning me?" I ask him, wondering when he'd decided to get so cocky.

That's not his role. His job is to follow orders, and he's doing a piss poor job of it.

"If there's anything I can do, I'll do it," he tells me. "If you need me to go to the hospital, I can."

"It wouldn't be hard," I explain. "You'd put on a pair of scrubs and walk in, steal a badge, find a room, pull a cord."

There's a pause, and I wonder what he is thinking.

"I'll do anything," he says. "Your will be done, Father."

A surge of pride wells through me. Even if the guys failed at bringing the five girls home in one piece, they're still loyal. That means something. That means a lot.

"You just need to stay the course," I say. "If I need you to get to the hospital and do something drastic, I'll let you know."

"Who's there now?"

"I have my sources."

But I don't reveal who my source is. I don't want the people in my fold to know my network. An important part of running this congregation is having complete respect. If they know I'm paying a nurse under the table to keep me posted, I don't think I would keep in their good graces. I'm not going to explain myself.

"It will all be over soon," I tell him. "Order will be restored. Do you hear me?"

"I do," he says.

"Then you tell me when you finish your mission. It should have already been over." I don't fight to hide the frustration in my voice. I run a hand through my slicked back hair. "She should be here. Now. She is a single woman, living alone, it shouldn't be so difficult. She was always weak, anyways."

"Tomorrow," he says. "I promise."

25 WILLOW

I HAVE NEVER in my life been hungover like this. I'm running late, which is something I never, ever am. I know that's a lot of nevers, but my word, my head is pounding.

When I woke up this morning, my throat was so dry. I chugged a glass of water, then another, took four ibuprofen, and prayed for a miracle. Now I feel like I need more than a miracle. I need to go back to bed.

Before I head out to the trail for my class, I need to grab some lecture notes that I'd printed to pass out to the class. We don't usually work with paper like that, but I thought we could go to a covered area on the trail, sit at some picnic benches, and go over the material.

There's no Wi-Fi that far out in the woods, so this would be a nice change of pace. I rush into my office and grab the papers from my desk, and as I'm darting out the door and heading down the hallway, I bump into Dean Clarence, walking with the president. Of course they're together. I stop in front of them, and they in front of me. He gives me a once-over and makes a comment after checking his watch. "Isn't your lecture at nine AM? It's nine-ten."

The way he speaks to me makes my skin crawl. Just who exactly does this man think he is?

"Look," I say. "I'm great at my job, and I'd be even better without your interference."

But still, as I walk away, it's hard to shake the words from our last conversation, when he'd scolded and told me I was on thin ice. My head is buzzing as I race toward the trailhead, hating that I'm now fifteen minutes late for my own lecture. Everyone is waiting for me.

"Hey," I address my students. "I'm sorry." I jog the last bit toward them. Everyone's already there. But as I scan the group, I notice Connor didn't make it. Still, that doesn't exactly surprise me, not after all the alcohol we'd consumed last night.

I'm guessing he skipped class so he could sleep it off himself. I'd be lying if I said I wasn't jealous. "Didn't think you were going to come," Caroline says. "Is everything all right? You're never late."

I groan. "I'm sorry, guys. It was just one of those mornings."

Joshua makes a joke. "Thirsty Thursday, huh?" It gets a chuckle from the rest of the class.

I meet my class with a telling expression, causing further laughter to erupt. "I am here now, so let's just take a shorter walk today instead of the full four-mile loop. I was thinking we could go over some printouts under that covered seating area."

"Sounds good to me," Caroline says. "I think it's going to rain anyways."

But before we make it out of the trail head, I notice several students looking at their phones. It's unusual because they all know that this class is tech-free.

"Is everything all right?" I ask not wanting to pry, but also wondering why their devices are still out. Usually by the time everyone reaches the trailhead, they've tucked their phones away and are ready to pay attention with focus.

"Actually," Sarah says. "Did you see the news?"

I frown. "No, I haven't."

Sarah tells me the breaking news. "They located a girl in the woods out in Hyacinth River."

"How far is that from here?" Joshua asks.

"Forty minutes maybe?" she answers.

Caroline nods. "Yeah, maybe thirty-five. It's about the halfway point between here and Seattle, but it's pretty remote."

"I've never been there," I say, "but you said they found a girl?" My mind is reeling.

Last night, Holt told me he had been out at Hyacinth River all day.

That means when he showed up at my house looking like a mess with his clothes wet and dirty, his eyes so tired after missing our date, he'd been working a case that had gotten very complicated, very quickly. He'd said as much, but I hadn't put the pieces together. Hadn't been able to, until now.

"Yeah," Caroline replies. "She's thirteen, and another girl was found dead. I guess the girl who was alive was helicoptered out."

"Oh my God," I say, realizing that Holt had just come from a long and traumatic day only to find me with another man.

I don't want to let on about my involvement with the lead investigator, but immediately Caroline asks me if I'm involved with the case.

"The FBI agent quoted in the article was the one you worked with on the last two cases, and he's listed as the primary investigator. Are you working with him on this one?"

I shake my head. "No. That case has not been brought to my attention. I only worked as a consultant on the other cases because they were related to cult affairs."

"Well, not just cult affairs," Joshua clarifies. "The Harmony case was sure, but Jackson Carter's daughter, Amy, wasn't in a cult."

"True," I say, "but she had been brainwashed and conditioned to change her thinking patterns and believe her captor was a hero. That's why I was brought in on that case."

"How did this girl survive?" Caroline asks Sarah.

"It says she'd been in the woods for two days. I mean, it's November. Poor thing must have been frozen by the time they found her."

Caroline nods. "At least it hasn't been raining."

I listen to them discuss the current event, and I realize that some of the information presented by the students parallels my own escape.

Obviously, I'm not going to explain that to them. I don't want them to know my history, but I take this teachable moment for what it is. "I don't know what or who the girls were escaping from and why one was found alive and the other dead. But I do know that when we are in our most terrified state, people can have a charge of adrenaline, a kick inside our subconscious that tells us to move, to go, to fight, and to survive. It sounds like that's what happened with her."

My students continue to flip their phones around to show me the scene of the helicopter pulling the girl from the woods below. Since I was already late and this whole conversation has taken over our class hour and hike, I decide to pause the coursework for today and instead hand out the materials I had printed.

"Read these over. Everyone can post what they think on the message board. I'm not feeling great, and this news is a lot."

"Is it a lot because the FBI agent didn't tell you about it?" Caroline asks with a grin.

I roll my eyes playfully. "I'm not discussing that. And no, it's just been ... Well, it just is what it is."

I try to chuckle it off, but inside I admit to feeling like crap for the way I treated Holt last night, assuming the worst when he'd just been fighting for the best for everybody else. He doesn't need someone getting mad at him. He needs support, regardless of whether I'm his partner, his girl-friend, or even just his friend. He deserves someone who believes in his best intention.

Class breaks up and I begin walking back toward my office. When I am near the building, I see Holt, leaning against the weathered facade. He's in a suit and tie with a raincoat on.

It throws me off seeing him here, and I notice that Caroline and Joshua turn and see Agent Holt. Then Caroline looks at me, her eyebrows raised, questioning if I just gave them lies in class, if I really am involved in the case.

But I wasn't lying.

Caroline and Joshua walk over to him before I could get there first. "You're Agent Holt, right?" Caroline asks. "I was wondering if you knew why five girls were kidnapped from Seattle neighborhoods the same after-noon. Is there a reason they were targeted specifically?"

"It's an ongoing investigation," he tells her simply, releasing an awkward chuckle. "So I can't speak about it. Sorry."

"Thanks, Caroline, for the question," I tell her. "I'll see you later." The way I phrase it is so pointed she can't help but walk away, yet she's still smirking as she turns around. I roll my eyes and turn to Holt. "I was not expecting to see you."

He rubs his jaw. He looks exhausted. His eyes are still red. "Can we catch up? I really am sorry about last night. I'm trying to be a good friend to you."

"Friend, huh?"

"I don't know, Willow. I'm just trying, is all, and I keep messing up. I want to apologize for last night and I tried to do that, but Connor was there and..."

"It's fine," I say. "You don't owe me anything."

He's scoffs. "I know I don't owe you anything, but I'm still your--" His phone buzzes and he pulls it out of his pocket. "Hello? Lucinda, what'd you find?" I can overhear the woman's voice. "All right, thanks. I appreciate it." He hangs up and turns to me once again. "I'm really sorry, but--"

My shoulders fall. "You need another rain check?" I want to be closer with Holt, but I don't know the right words to say, how to let him know how I feel.

He nods. "Yeah. Victim one, Chelsea, regained consciousness and is able to talk. I need to get over to the hospital to see what I can gather."

"Oh gosh, okay," I say, knowing none of this is about me. His work is so important, lives are literally at stake. " Do you want me to come along?"

He frowns. "No, you're not needed. Not because I don't want to be around you, but ... Well, this is my case." He wears a defeated expression, then leans in to give me a hug, but it feels awkward enough to remind me of the fragile state of our relationship. "I'll call you later. I promise."

But as I watch him go, it's impossible not to wonder if his words carry any weight at all. What his promises really mean.

26 HOLT

SINCE HYACINTH RIVER is closer to Olympia than Seattle, Chelsea was taken there after her rescue last night. I'm grateful Lucinda called to let me know that she had regained consciousness, and I'm hoping when I get to the hospital, she'll be willing to talk. At the moment, I have no leads to go on. And while I have Jedd working through the list of white vans, that effort is going slow.

I need something now, something tangible. I'm hoping Chelsea will at least be able to identify the men who'd abducted her. That would help me get closer to finding the other three girls, to bring justice to them all. And as much as I am grateful that I can get to the hospital quickly, I can't help but feel shitty about the way I'd left Willow once again.

The sky is overcast and gray as I drive to the hospital. The weather puts me in a reflective mood, and I can't help but think about where I am in life, and why.

The work hours I have is exactly why I've never had a relationship, why I've always kept women at arm's length, because my life's work doesn't mesh well with consistency.

How can I be on call, working a case around the clock, and also be there for a girlfriend? Because in the end, I'm always going to choose work – it's not like I'm doing work that can wait. Every case I take on is urgent. I'm trying to make the world a better, safer place and we're talking about lives, real lives on the line. And even though most women would say they understand that, that they get how important my job is, how important this work is -- deep down, everyone deserves a lover who can show up consistently for them.

When I get to the hospital and up to the waiting room closest to Chelsea's room, I find Leroy McGavin, Chelsea's father. "Good to see you again, Agent Holt," he says, shaking my hand firmly.

He's tall and muscular, lean. His eyes are clear. I like this man. "You too. In the brief, I read that you were an Army Ranger."

He nods. "I was."

"Thank you for your service," I say to him.

He gives me a terse look and starts us on a slow trek down the hall. "Thank you for yours."

"I think your daughter is pretty lucky to have a dad like you."

"Oh, yeah?" he asks, running a hand over his jaw. " I'm pretty lucky to have a girl like her. Her mom passed a few years ago, and well, Chels, she's my whole world. I was scared, so scared I was going to lose her too. I can't help but think I'm a terrible parent for letting her get taken. I tried to teach her, Agent Holt, I tried to show her the ropes, how to prepare herself for worst-case scenarios, and then look, she got abducted from our own neighborhood. How did I let that happen?"

"Hey," I say. The hospital is bustling around us, but we move to stand in a quieter corner, pausing our walk. "You can't beat yourself up for what you did or did not do. You're an amazing father, incredible on all accounts, and your daughter wouldn't be here right now if you hadn't taught her how to survive in the wild. I'm guessing you're the one who taught a thirteen-year-old how to start a fire without so much as a match or a stick of flint."

Tears filled man's eyes. I saw him inhale and look away in attempt to keep them from falling. " I mean, I wanted her to know how to take care of herself." He looked down at his feet and shook his head. "I just feel like I dropped the ball."

"No," I say, "You were smart and I know that because your girl is smart. She survived in the woods for two days on her own after seeing another girl die. Whatever you taught her hit home. Maybe more people need to have fathers like you."

"Thank you," he says, his eyes meeting mine again. "I mean it."

"Look, I've heard that Chelsea just woke up and I respect her need for privacy, but I was wondering if there's any chance you could let me talk to her about what happened. If she can give us any indication of who took her, any clues or identifying factors of her abductors."

Leroy hesitates for a moment. "She's still pretty out of it right now, but you could try to talk to her," he says. "We've got to find those other three girls. We can't let them..." His words trail off.

I finish his sentence. "They deserve to be found."

"I'll do my best to help you," he tells me. "I can help facilitate a conversation, but she hasn't been saying much yet. Mostly one syllable or strings of words here and there."

I nod in understanding, then complete the short walk into the hospital room with Leroy. Chelsea is lying in bed, blankets bundling her like a cozy burrito. Her eyes are closed. Leroy steps to her and kneels beside the bed, taking her hand in his. "Hey, baby girl," he says. "This is Agent Holt." Her eyes open slowly at the sound of her father's voice. "He needs your help. They're trying to find the men who took you. Can you tell us anything about it? Anything about that afternoon?"

Her eyes fill with tears and one droplet rolls down her cheek. For a girl who's so damn strong and made it on her own out there, she's also a child who's been through a traumatic experience.

"I—" Chelsea's voice squeaks and scratches. "I can't. I can't. I..." Her lips press tight. Her chin quivers. She rolls over to one side and begins to cry.

Immediately, I regret not bringing Willow along with me. I try again, but once more, I reach an impasse. Chelsea's refusing to speak. It's why Willow should have been here. She's an expert on helping people speak their truth.

There's no way this girl's going to talk to me, and Leroy must feel the same way. "I promise to keep working with her," he says. "If I get anywhere, I'll call you right away. But she's going to be released from the hospital this afternoon, so I won't be calling you from here. I'll be able to call you from home."

I shake his hand and wish him well. "Before I go, though," I add, " I know someone who's an expert in this. Someone who has been able to help victims to speak about their trauma. Maybe next time I come out to see Chelsea, I could bring her with me."

"Of course," he says. "I want my daughter to be well, that's what matters the most."

I get back in my car after leaving the hospital. I realize I now have to eat crow as I head back toward the campus that I just left. I need Willow's assistance. The assistance she offered, that I refused.

Damn it. I can't help but kick myself for being so damn dumb. I let my personal feelings cloud my judgment on this case. If I wouldn't have been thinking about the tug of war I'm having with Willow right now, I would've brought her with me without a second thought. Now, I'm returning to her once more, asking for forgiveness, telling her I'm sorry.

27 WILLOW

AFTER HOLT both came and left so unexpectedly, I decided to take my mind off him and refocus on my work. I sit at my desk and pull up my inbox. I have several emails from students to reply to and a few messages from past clients. I hate having my inbox full, so I begin to work through them. After twenty minutes of pounding away at my keyboard and hitting the send button on repeat, I'm down to only half a dozen left when there's a knock on my office door.

"Come in," I say, wrapping up the current message.

Malcolm pokes his head in. "Hey, am I interrupting?"

"No, it's fine." I tear my gaze away from the screen. "It's been a while since I've seen you."

He pauses for a moment, studying me. "You look like..."

I laugh. "What?"

"I don't know. Maybe like you need a break?"

"Do I look that bad?" I joke.

Malcolm grins. "I wouldn't say bad. You kind of look stressed. Like maybe you need a drink."

At the mere thought of it, I feel my stomach rumble. "That's the last thing I need right now."

He frowns. "Is everything okay? I'm asking just as a friend. I realize that's where we're at these days."

I cringe. "Sorry, Malcolm. Did I make things weird before?"

"No," he says. "We're good, Willow. I promise."

"All right." I hope he is being honest.

"But I mean it," he says. "Do you need anything?"

"No. I'm doing all right. Just trying to get through emails and I feel like when I delete one, another one comes in."

He chuckles. "I understand. I've been there myself."

"You know I actually have one of your students. He just transferred into my class, Connor Wheeler. He said he used to be pre-law."

"Huh," he says, folding his arms across his chest. "I know your classes are very popular, so I'm not surprised he'd prefer to be in your classroom. Or on a trail with you."

I laugh. "Anyway, I appreciate the offer for a drink, but it's definitely not the time. Last night I had way too much."

"You did?" Malcolm seems surprised. "I don't think I've ever even seen you finish a glass of wine."

I sigh. " I don't know what came over me." I rub my temples.

As I do, a new email lands in my inbox. Connor's name fills in the "From" line.

Sorry I missed your class today. I'm sure it was great. Too much of the red wine left me under the weather. Maybe you could catch me up on it later. No booze this time. How about I stop by with coffee?

"Just a second, Malcolm," I say. "I need to respond to this real quick."

I email Connor back. *Thanks, but I'm going to take a rain check on that.* I'm not trying to be rude, but the truth is, I want a little space from Connor. After all, I am his teacher and inviting him to my home was probably the least appropriate thing I've ever done in my life. I almost confide in Malcolm about it, but before I can, another email hits my inbox. Another one from Connor.

I'd like to talk to you about a relic from my past that might be the key to providing closure for you and yours.

I frown.

"What is it?" Malcolm asks.

"Nothing," I say, closing my laptop, having no idea what that might mean. But Connor's message compels me to leave for the day. I'm exhausted, and I'm tired of thinking about my past. And I know whatever was going on last night with Connor was just one thing too much. I move to stand and pack my bag for the day, the transition making me woozy and unstable.

Malcom rushes in to steady me. "Are you sure everything's all right?"

"Yeah, I just have a headache. Just need to go home and close my eyes."

"All right," he says. "Honestly, if you need anything at all, I'm here for you."

"I know, Malcolm, and I appreciate it." I slide my laptop into my messenger bag. A part of me wants to tell Malcolm more, but I'm leery about telling him more about Connor and his past. The last time a student crossed the line with me, it resulted in Malcolm's TA getting the boot.

Malcolm and I leave the office together and I lock it up.

"I hope your hangover doesn't last too long, Willow," Malcolm says with a grin.

I groan. "God. Me too."

I leave campus and get in my car. Before I pull out of the parking lot, I send Holt a quick text. *It was nice to see you this morning.*

I leave it at that because it *was* nice to see him and, honestly, at this point I'm not sure what else to say. He's been hot and cold and leaving me confused.

And right now, I just want something that makes sense.

28 FLINT

"I DON'T CARE what you want," I tell him. "I care about reclaiming what belongs to us."

"I understand that," he tells me. "I do. It's just..." His words trail off.

"It's just what?" I say back into the phone. I'm pacing my office. The lightbulb in the overhead fixture flickers, the room is cold. There is a sense of doom with each additional hour we lose waiting. "We have plans, plans for a ceremony, a reckoning, and if everyone isn't present, it's not going to work, not in the way it's been ordained, the way I have written it in our book of prayers, in our book of truth!"

"I know I need to get her there."

"Chelsea has been released from the hospital," I tell him. "Which means she's at her home now, and I'm going to need your assistance to ensure things go smoothly. The past incompetence has really caused me to question your ability."

"What's the timeline?" he asks me. "Because I'm trying. I just..."

"I don't want any more *just*s, and I don't want any more trying. Do I need to send someone else out to help you?"

"No. I can do it."

"Are you sure? Because we cannot mess this up. Everyone here is planning on the ceremony happening tonight. It was the date that the Lord told me it would occur. All people should have already been present. It's because of your incompetence that we're waiting on the missing puzzle piece. Is that how callously you see the Lord's desire, how you want to honor the prophecy?"

"Of course not," he says, "Of course not, Father Flint. I will make it happen. Whatever you need, I'll do."

"I think I'm going to send out Benjamin to help you execute the plan."

"You don't trust me?" he asks. "I have only ever been faithful to you."

"Faithful, yes. But it's not like you've exactly shown yourself capable, and I don't want anyone else gone from the compound tonight."

"It won't be tonight. I'll be there sooner than that, I promise."

"You gave me promises yesterday too. Chelsea's not back yet, is she?"

"I know," he says. "Your will will be done. I mean it, Father."

I end the call with a wave of righteous anger burning through me. As a leader, I have people looking up to me, counting on my prophecies to be their salvation. I wrote this all down months ago when I devised the plan, when I saw the vision, when I knew what needed to happen, and I truly believed I could count on my closest men, my allies, to help me carry it out. Now, I question their ability. And now is not the time for me to start doubting anybody. I need this to reveal itself as it was written.

If the members of my fold show up at the ceremony tonight and all the components of the prophecy are not accounted for, I will look like a heretic, a false prophet, and I cannot let that happen, not after everything I've worked to build.

I've spent the last thirty years of my life creating this heaven on earth. This was supposed to be the fulfillment, the full circle. It was supposed to be the culmination, the ultimate sacrifice, having someone who has strayed return to us, then offer her to God on the altar of life. I cannot be made into a fool, not because of the incompetence of my men, no. I pick up the phone and call him again.

He doesn't answer, and I leave a voicemail. This time, my voice is filled with the fury of a thousand swords.

"You will not fail me. If you do, you will forever regret it. I will hunt you down and I will carve out your heart and I will put it on that altar. You will be a living sacrifice. I hope you understand that when I say this. I'm speaking nothing but the word of God. I am speaking nothing but the truth. And the truth shall set you free."

29 AGENT HOLT

I know it doesn't look great pulling back up to Conifer College. This time I am here to apologize – once more -- and then ask for a favor immediately after.

I'm hoping Willow understands.

The case I've been working on has been hellish, and we seem no closer to an end than we did yesterday. Rob has sent me an update letting me know that there is no evidence of others out along the river. No other girls have been found. Jedd and Lucinda from the bureau also let me know that they've been working through the van list but haven't gotten any closer to a lead.

I'm glad I'm working this case with Smith. He's the kind of guy I can problem-solve with, but he isn't with the with FBI and there are limits to our partnership. That makes me wish I wasn't always flying solo. Maybe I need to ask Tamara to get me a partner. I pull out my phone as I walk toward Willow's office, and I see that a half an hour ago she texted me.

It was nice to see you this morning.

I smile, grateful that she's not mad at me at the very least. I text a reply. *I'm here now.*

When I get to her office, though, no one answers my knock. I frown. I send a second text. *I'm here. Are you?*

Standing in the empty hallway, I debate what I should do when I see

Malcolm appear. It's a little bit awkward when I reintroduce myself, but Malcolm just shakes it off.

"Honestly, we don't need to be weird," he tells me. "I know you have a thing with Willow and she doesn't have a thing for me."

I chuckle. "I wasn't going to say any of that."

"I know, but it's what you were thinking," Malcolm says.

Ignoring the line of conversation, I ask, "Actually, do you know where Willow is? I was hoping to catch her. Could really use her expertise on a case."

"I don't think she's here," he tells me. "But you should know, I think she's been having a hard time."

"Really?" I ask. "How so?"

"I've heard she's on thin ice with the department head and the president because of all the press and involvement with these investigations. Honestly, it seems like Willow is working more for the FBI than the university. Maybe you should just hire her full-time."

"Willow loves teaching. She will be devastated if she loses her job that she's worked so hard for."

"She does, but, damn, she sure as hell rushed out of here earlier today. A few minutes ago, actually. She said she had something she needed to take care of at home." Malcolm shrugs. "Maybe it's something about one of her private sessions or something. I don't know. She was off. I think she was hungover."

I run a hand over my jaw. Malcolm is giving me all the information he has. I wonder why. "What's your angle here?" I ask him. "Why are you giving me the rundown on Willow?"

He shrugs. "I don't know. She's my friend. She doesn't seem herself. I didn't know if you knew why. She wouldn't really give a straight answer."

"I wish I knew, but honestly we haven't seen one another much lately."

Malcolm nods. " I keep inviting her to trivia night and she blows me off, so it's not just you."

I laugh good-naturedly even though the reason Willow and I haven't connected is because I'm the one blowing her off, even if unintentionally. "Do you work in this wing?" I ask him. "I thought you were a law professor."

Malcolm nods. "I don't, and yeah, I am. I was just stopping by to see Willow. I had forgotten that I needed to tell her something earlier."

"I see." My phone rings and I pull it out of my pocket. I see it's Lucinda from the office. I hold up one finger and take the call. Malcolm waits.

"Hey, Holt. So Leroy just called. He said Chelsea's willing to speak with you."

"That's great," I tell her. "I'm on my way now. I was actually trying to find Willow Grace."

"Willow?" Luciana says. "Why?"

"Remember she helped me with the last two cases I led. I could use her help getting Chelsea to open up."

"All right. Well, that makes sense," Luciana says, but her voice feels a little more clipped.

"Thanks for the update."

"Yeah, of course," Luciana says. "I just wanted you to know that Leroy says they're home and I can forward you their address."

"Great," I say. "Again, I really appreciate it."

I end the call and try Willow's number. It goes straight to voicemail, which isn't unusual if she's at home. There's poor reception surrounding her cabin. Still, I send her a quick text.

Can you call me when you get this? I'd really like to borrow you for an interview. Let me know, but I'm headed your way. I'm really hoping you can help.

I press send on the text and then slide my phone back in my pocket. "I'm sorry, Malcolm. That was rude."

"No, it's fine," he says. "I know you're actually, like, solving murders." He grins when he says that using hand gestures and I shrug.

"Just doing my part. I know you are too."

Malcolm nods and looks around, as if something interesting were behind the cinderblock wall. "Hey, did you say you're on your way to see Willow now?" Malcolm asks.

"Yeah, I am. I was just going to head out since the only reason I came to Conifer College was to see her."

"Would you mind passing something on to her? It's the reason I was walking over here in the first place."

"Sure. What is it?" I appreciate Malcolm's camaraderie.

"Earlier, she'd mentioned a student who'd switched from the law program to psych. When she mentioned his name, it wasn't familiar. I'm great with statutes but terrible with names." I smile as he keeps speaking. "I did a quick check on him through the register, and there's no one listed by the name of Connor Wheeler."

Immediately a red flag goes up. In my mind, I'm not sure what this information means, but it sets my spider sense tingling down my back. Whatever it is, it isn't good.

"You're sure?" I ask. "Connor Wheeler isn't a student here?"

"No." Malcolm says. "Isn't currently and never has been."

"You just might be the person I was meant to see here after all," I say. "That information might just be exactly what I need."

30 WILLOW

I PULL up to my house and notice two vehicles in my driveway. I feel like I know one of them from somewhere but can't place it. The other is a big white van with a blue paint transfer on the fender. My heart begins pounding. I reach for my phone in the console, confused as to why I didn't get an alert of a security breach, but my cell signal is dead. Whoever found my property was smart enough to cut the Wi-Fi, rendering any notifications unsent.

As I put my car in park, I try to piece together who this might be. I don't want to jump to worst case scenarios, but at this point in my life, it's the only option I have. I've got to play it safe and be smart.

I get out of my car cautiously, wishing I kept a gun in my glove compartment. Instead, I walk over to the next best option: the ax lying next to my wood pile. I reach for the handle and bring the weapon to my shoulder, arming myself. I have no idea who might be waiting for me inside.

I walk up the steps, hating that I now feel fearful in my own home. I've worked so hard to make this place safe and now someone's broken in. Someone's found me. Just as I prepare to enter my front door, I hear a creak from behind me on the porch. I turn, bracing myself for whatever might come next and see a man I don't recognize. He has a white gauze bandage wrapped around his head, as if he'd been recently injured. I grimace at the sight of him. He's big and burly.

"Don't get any closer," I say.

I have the ax handle in both my hands, bracing it in front of me. I don't want to start swinging, but I will if I have to.

"I think it'd be best if you drop your weapon," he tells me.

"I don't know who you are. What are you doing here?"

"We came for Father."

I brace myself for my worst nightmare coming true, biting back the fear that has been gnawing at me for so many years, that one day I would be found.

"Father," I repeat. I shake my head, tears in my eyes. "No. No, no, no. I'm not going back there," I tell him. "I'm never going back there."

"Father Flint disagrees."

"Don't," I say. "Please don't. I don't want..."

But the door to my cabin opens and before I can run, a rag is forced to my nose. Chloroform. I world begins to fade to black and I push myself against his elbows, trying to break free through the door in my cabin. I see a body on the ground. A man has already been shot.

My eyes close. I don't know if I wish I would've gotten here ten minutes earlier or ten minutes later. Deep down, I wish I had never gotten here at all. My eyes and head spin, and I feel the men take hold of me, lifting me over their shoulders. I am carried away from my home, and my body falls like a thud as the wheels of the van begin to move.

My last thought as the darkness consumes me, is that I should have spoken up.

31 AGENT HOLT

WHEN I PULL up to Willow's house, I'm relieved to see her car there. But there's another car in the driveway. I remember it from the other night. I walk to the front door, bracing myself. The last thing I want to do is walk in on her and that guy Connor again.

It was brutal last time. I don't think I'm ready for a repeat less than twenty-four hours later.

But when I walk up the steps, my senses tingle again. I'm immediately on high alert. The door is open. There's an axe lying on the porch. I put my hand on my holster.

"Willow," I call out. "Willow Grace. It's Holt. Are you here?"

I step inside, pulling the gun out now and holding it in front of me with my right hand.

"Willow?"

But the moment I step inside the door, I'm stunned by what I see. The man I'd met just last night, who gave me such an uncomfortable feeling, whose name is not in the school's register, is lying here on the ground. Shot in the heart. Bleeding out on Willow Grace's floor.

I kneel in front of him. Connor Wheeler. Even though I now know that's not his real name. I take his wrist. He's dead obviously. No pulse. But his body is warm and if Willow only left campus a short time before me, it means everything that happened here happened quickly.

I stand, wanting to see if anything else is amiss. My stomach turns in fear, a knot of worry inside me.

The last thing I want is to find Willow dead too.

I scan Connor's body. He has no weapon, no gun on his person. I pat him down and make sure of it. He was unarmed.

The kitchen is empty. The living room too. Her office is locked shut, the padlock secure. Down the hall, the guest room has no signs of life. Bathroom, the same.

With my hand on her bedroom door handle I open it, bracing myself for whatever I might come across next. As an agent I've seen plenty of horrific things, but the idea of finding Willow dead in her bedroom might be one thing too many for me to bear.

When I open the door, though, relief floods me. The room is empty. Her bed is still made. This can only mean one other thing, though. Someone took her.

I walk toward the front of the house to the security system, realizing it has been disabled. Ripped from the wall. Completely destroyed. Goddammit.

I call my boss.

"Hello?" Tamara answers.

"I need a local contingent to work a scene here." I give her the rundown. The man who's dead, the cabin where I am.

"It's Willow Grace's house," I tell her.

"Oh God, how is she involved?"

"I don't know, but I'm going to find out. I really thought this guy, the one dead in her home... I really thought he was involved, but now I'm not so sure."

"All right," Tamara says. "I'll call in a team. Stay there until they arrive."

"Of course," I say. "I hope the handoff can happen quickly. I don't want to waste any time trying to find Willow."

"I know. Hang tight."

We end the call. Tamara knows that I have some sort of feelings for Willow, but as agents, we push our personal involvement down to do the work in front of us.

I hate that I have to remain on the scene long enough for the handoff, but I don't have a choice. While I wait, I decide to call Smith. I'm going to drag him in. Maybe I should have done that yesterday.

"Hey," he says, answering the phone after one ring. "What's up?"

I give him the details.

"You're at Willow's now?"

"Yeah," I say. "This guy is dead, and I thought he was the one who was after her. He's a total creep. I wish we knew who he really was so we could run a background check." An idea sparks and I decide to check for a wallet in his pockets. Bingo!. "Maybe we still can. Just found his wallet on him."

"Probably shouldn't have done that," Smith admonishes.

"I'm not here to waste time."

"Okay. What have you got?"

"His name's Craig Martin. At least that's what his driver's license says."

I give him the address listed on the license.

"All right, I'll have my guys run this," he says. "Do you want me to meet you out at Willow's?"

"Yeah, but where are you?"

"I'm about forty minutes out."

"All right," I say. "I think I'll be here as long as that. I have to wait till the local jurisdiction shows up to deal with Craig Martin."

"Any idea where Willow might have gone?"

"I have one guess," I say. "Her past was messy. She was in some sort of cult, but I don't know the name or even where it's located. But she's always looking over her shoulder, always scared." I run a palm down my face. "Dammit. Bringing her into that case with Amy Carter is probably what put her in the limelight. She was so distraught about having her picture in the paper."

Smith whistles low. "So, if the cult who had her captive were able to identify where she was now, they could be pulling her back in."

"Exactly," I say.

"Any idea what this group was and where it was located?" Smith asks.

"No," I say. "But now that I think of it, I'm going to go look in her office and see if I can find any clues."

"All right," Smith says. "I'll see you soon."

We end the call and I walk to the padlocked office. But I don't have a key to unlock it. Then I remember the axe on the front porch.

I go back for it, gripping the heavy weapon with two hands, and walk back into the house and down the hall. "Sorry, Willow," I say out loud as I gear up to break and enter her most sacred space. Then, with a heavy hand, I slam the sharp metal against the lock. Right now, there's something more important than keeping her past private: Keeping her future intact.

Her office is a strange and marvelous place. Bookshelves line the walls. A desk that sits in front of a large window peering into her section of the woods is messy, full of highlighted papers and tabbed out research. Post-it Notes on the wall, a bulletin board tacked full of articles and maps and clippings.

I go through her files in the first folder I find. It lists all the different groups she's been connected to over the years. She has spent a decade doing work that's so damn meaningful. The information in this office alone is exemplary.

At the very back of the file cabinet is a sealed, unlabeled manila envelope, standing out from the rest. I pull it out and run my finger under the seal, opening it. A stack of papers, photographs, and pages of notes are inside.

I immediately recognize Willow's image in the first photograph of the stack. She's standing with a man in a collared shirt and tie. She's in a long, simple dress, her dark hair in a braid. She looks at least fifteen years younger. Her eyes are hollow and sad. She has a tight smile on her face. They're standing in front of a sign that says Fountain of Faith. Surrounding them are seventy or eighty people, all ages. I'm assuming it's the fold. *Fountain of Faith.* I've never heard of this group before, but I begin to learn about them quickly as I read Willow's notes.

Escaping wasn't easy, but I planned my move for years. I saved money from every trip we took to Walmart. And even though I knew I would be severely punished if the money was found, I kept it hidden in the floorboard underneath my bed. Thankfully Father Flint didn't require me to sleep with him each night, and even though I was his only wife, even though other brothers of the fold engaged in polygamy, I had my own sleeping quarters.

I sometimes wondered if he slept with other women, and I'm sure he did, but he never took another as a wife. I never questioned what he did because, honestly, if he wanted to sleep with anyone besides me, I was fine with it. I never wanted to sleep with him at all. He's twice my age and when we married, I was only 16 years old. I didn't want to be linked to him in any way, but he had had his eyes set on me since I was young. I knew that.

Everyone knew that. He thought I was his holy partner. In bed he would call me his twin flame and I never understood what that meant. But he said we were divinely appointed by the Father in heaven.

And for a while I believed it. I thought maybe I truly was a gift from the Lord on high for Flint. But then the more I got to know him, Flint, I realized how duped I had been. He was manipulating me because he was not a prophet. He was just a man. I saw how weak he was, how tormented he was, how he was unable to get me pregnant. And I know it wasn't because of my body. I know it was because of his. Because later, after we'd been married for years, he attempted to procreate with other women in the fold. Not because he loved them, he promised me that. No, because he needed to carry on the prophecy in which he'd been told that he would have five daughters, and if I couldn't bear him one, maybe someone else could. But it was the same with them as it was with me. None of the women were the issue. Flint was.

My heart sinks to my stomach as I set the note down and look out the window. Before I lose all composure, I reach for a hand-drawn map Willow had made. It's a map of Washington State, marking the Fountain of Faith's actual location. It's not too far away on the Washington coast, outside of Aberdeen.

I frown. I suppose if it was in a remote enough location between there, no one would even be looking for them, wondering about them. That's how so many small groups like this can stay under the radar.

In my gut, I know they've taken her back.

But now I have a map, which means Smith and I, we're sure as hell going to find her.

32 CHELSEA

"Do you need anything?" Dad asks.

I'm cozy on the couch with my favorite blankets and stuffies. He has the remote on the coffee table in case I want the TV on. And he's just made me a hot cocoa with marshmallows, my favorite. "I'm good, Dad," I say. "I'm just so happy I'm home."

"Me too, sweetheart. I have never been so scared." I can tell he's starting to well up and holding it back. It's not something he does often.

My dad is a strong, silent type of man. He's tough as nails and hard as hell, and that's why I think he's the best guy in the whole world. He would do anything for the people he loves. I know he would do anything for me, even if that meant putting himself in danger. I'm just so thankful that nothing bad had to happen to him for me to get back home.

"You're so strong," he says. "You're strong enough to get through anything after that." He sits down on the couch next to me and wraps an arm around my shoulders.

"I was scared though, Dad. I know you think I was strong, but I don't think I'm as tough as you think. I started crying one night because I heard these coyotes and I just... I thought they were going to get me."

Dad pulled me in tighter, closer. "That is one situation where it's okay to cry. You pulled through. Thank God Agent Holt was the one out there looking for you. I just can't believe you had to go through that."

I tilt my head in order to look up at him. "You know that girl, Ruby?" I say. "The one who died? She was trying so hard to be brave. There were five of us in that van you know, and only her and I were willing to leap when we had the chance, so I don't know what happened to the other girls. I should have done something more. I should have fought more for them. I just--"

"Sweetheart, don't do that. You did everything you could."

Before I could start crying again, there's a knock on the door. I didn't think we were expecting anything, but Dad stands and replaces the pillows behind my head.

"Maybe it's the food I ordered," he tells me, grinning like a madman. "I got you pepperoni pizza."

I smile back. "You never order junk food. Hot cocoa and pizza in one day? Did someone replace your brain with someone else's while I was gone, Dad?" We're an *ingredients-we-can-pronounce* type of house. Rice and beans and nuts and granola, almond milk, that kind of thing. So junk food like this is a real treat. But when Dad answers the door, he raises his voice.

"I don't know what you're doing here, but you need to go."

"No," a man's voice says. "We're not going anywhere. We're exactly where we're meant to be."

"Look, I don't want any trouble. I don't know why--"

"I don't really care what you want. I'm here for her. I'm coming back for what is ours."

My eyes widen and I burrow myself under the blankets. I recognize that voice.

I don't want to see those men again. I immediately pull back. I have to make sure Dad's okay. I quietly hop off the couch and tip toe in a low crouch.

"No," he says, "You've got to go. I don't know what you're getting at, but you're not coming in my home."

"And what do you think you're going to do to stop me?"

Hovering near the hallway between the living room and foyer, the man I struck with that tire rod is standing in the doorway of our house. His head is bandaged, and when his eyes find mine, his glare sends a straight line of terror through my body.

"Do you want to die?" he hisses to Dad. "I think it's time you step back."

"No, don't hurt him," I whimper.

My dad though pushes the man away. "Don't get any closer," Dad demands.

"Derrick," the driver says to the man with the bandaged head, "Get her. I'll take care of him."

The man I hurt walks toward me, I run back to the couch. He leaps over the couch and grabs my wrists.

"Let me go," I scream, "Please, let me go. Let me go!"

"I'm not letting you go," he growls, swinging me up over his shoulder.

Dad tries to get to him, but the other man pulls him back. I'm crying, shouting for my father.

"Don't want you to get hurt, Dad. Don't do anything that could get you hurt."

Derrick pulls out his gun and shoots my father. I scream. My voice curdles like blood. I watch as his body falls to the floor, crying in agony. He wasn't armed. He couldn't protect himself.

"I love you, Chels," he groans in pain, holding his body, blood pouring out, seeping through his gray t-shirt.

My whole body feels like a river rock floating to the bottom. I feel like a dead weight, empty, like nothing. My whole body begins to shake as the fight is taken out of me.

"Run, Chels," he says. My father's voice. Are those his last words? He doesn't say anything else. His eyes are closed. And I try to push away from the man who holds me tight, but I can't get out of his grip. I smash my fists against his back. I kick him as hard as I can into his chest. "Just let me go," I scream. "Let me go. Daddy, Daddy, don't go!" I sob as I'm carried out of my home and thrown back into the van. All I wanted was to stay home with my dad. And now, once again, I'm being hauled away to a future that is so wildly unknown, and so terribly alone.

33 WILLOW

It's impossible to try and orient myself to my surroundings. I don't know what time it is, if it's early or late, if it's been a day or more, but my body is vibrating from the motion under me.

I open my eyes, trying to sit upright, realizing both my ankles and my wrists are bound. I'm in a van. The windows are all blacked out, but I'm not alone. I feel someone next to me even if I can't see them.

"I tried to wake you up," the girl says, her voice low. There are two men in the front of the van, but music is on, and they seem lost in conversation. "You've been asleep for like an hour and I didn't know where we were and I didn't know what to do and--"

"Hey, hey, it's okay," I say. I realize there's a young girl in this van with me. It's just the two of us in the back. "I'm sorry. I think I was drugged. I don't know where I am either. I don't know what's happening." I rub my now-throbbing head. "I'm sorry I can't help."

"I know some things," the girl says. There's a slice of light beneath one of the windows that isn't blacked out. The light streams across her face, a soft glow, brown eyes, dark hair. A younger me.

"I'm Chelsea," she says.

"Hi, Chelsea," I say, sitting up. "I'm Willow, Willow Grace. You think you know where we are?" I ask her.

She shakes her head.

My own head pounds. I'm trying to remember what happened before. Images wash around me as I remember getting to my house, the axe in my hand, the men, their words. *Father Flint.* A chill runs over my body.

"I know where we're going," I tell her.

"You do?" she asks. "Because this is the second time these men have kidnapped me and--"

"Truly?" I say in a whisper, not wanting to get the attention of the men up front. "What do you mean?"

"A few days ago, three days ago, I was walking home from school and these guys, Benjamin and Derrick, they came after me and put me in this van and there were four other girls. That made five of us altogether, and then at some point there was a flat tire or something and I was able to convince one of the girls, Ruby, to help try and attack the guys and so we were able to escape, but then..." Chelsea starts to sob.

"Hey, it's okay, it's okay," I say. "Come here." She's bound too, but somehow we're able to scooch ourselves together, sitting side by side, hip to hip on the cold floor of the van. "It's okay," I say, "Just get it all out as best you can."

She begins speaking through muffled sobs, doing her best to not alert the men up front. "We were running through the woods. Ruby fell, and I told her to get up, that we can get through this together. I really thought we could make it. We kept running and we got to this cliff. It was a dead end, below there was a river," she says, tears falling down her cheek, her chin. "And I thought we could make it. I did. I jumped far and I fell into that river and it was ice-cold, but I came up breathing. But Ruby, she didn't jump the same as I did. She got caught on the way down, and she fell on the shore. She died. I watched her die .... she's dead ... it's because she followed me."

My heart ached for this girl next to me. She's so young and has already seen too much. "You can't blame yourself. You did the best you could."

But tears roll down Chelsea's cheeks. "I told her to get out of the van and if she had stayed in the van, she would still be alive. And it's all my fault... It's all my fault, and now I'm back in the van. And it's probably my punishment because I'm the reason Ruby died. It's all my fault."

"Nothing is your fault," I say, realizing that this girl is the child Holt rescued, the girl in the helicopter. My heart goes out to her, realizing just how much she's been through in such a short amount of time. Oh my

God, this poor child. "See, you are strong," I say. "You made it out of the woods."

"I was rescued after two days. I thought I was going to die, but I didn't. But then I got home from the hospital." At this point, she's completely sobbing. Her whole body is shaking, trembling, and I can't wrap an arm around her because my hands are tied together and all I want to do is give this child a hug and tell her it's going to be okay. Even though I know where we're going. I know it's *not* going to be okay. "Did you know the men?"

"Not before they came for me. But why did they come for you?" she asks.

I swallow. "I think these are men from my past."

"You're friends with them?"

"No, not like that. I used to be a part of a group. When I was a child, my mother, she and I moved there and I was only seven or eight. But I lived there until I was twenty-one, until I escaped."

She wipes at her face with her bound hands and asks, "Your mom took you to a bad group?"

"Not on purpose. She thought it was a good place to go. That it would be safe. She didn't have money. She thought this was the best thing for us, for her and me."

"But they were bad, these people?"

I nod. "They were very bad."

"Why do they want you back?"

"I don't know," I say, but I know that's not entirely true.

I have ideas of why they want me back, why *he* wants me back. He had always told everyone that I was a fulfillment of his prophecy and me leaving the fold would mean that he was a liar, a fraud, a fake. But he must have somehow convinced these people in the nearly fifteen years since I've been gone that it's a story of a prodigal son, that I'm on my way home, that I always have been.

I don't tell this to Chelsea. It's not the right time. "How old are you?" I ask her.

"Thirteen," she whispers.

"And the other girls, how old were they?"

"We all seemed about the same age. We kind of look the same too. We all have the same color of hair and eyes. It's kind of weird, huh?"

I swallow. I look down at my clothes for the first time. "Oh my God," I say.

"What?" she asks.

After they drugged me, they must have changed me into this.

"I was wondering," Chelsea says, following my gaze with her own. "Wondering why you're wearing that dress."

"It's what they call a wedding dress," I whisper.

"It doesn't look very fancy for a wedding."

"Nothing there is very fancy."

Fountain of Faith was a group that believed in going back to the basics and fending for themselves, taking care of their own. They dressed in simple clothing and made most of it themselves. They farmed and canned and had stables and a dairy. They only went to town when they needed to, a Walmart mostly. But it was a big trip and they'd only go there for items they couldn't make on their own, like coffee, sugar, flour, surprises for the children. But it was rare and we never went without supervision.

Obviously, I don't explain all of that to Chelsea, and I hope it's never information she really needs to understand, because, hopefully, this will be over before she gets indoctrinated into the teachings of the Fountain of Faith.

"Don't worry," she tells me. "I know you seem really sad right now, but..." She wipes her eyes, her tears are gone. She sits up straighter her shoulders back. "But I have to be strong, because I just watched my dad die and I've already lost my mom and I can't have my story end like that, like this. I'm strong, Willow Grace."

I look at this girl, a younger version of me. "Yes, you are, Chelsea. You're absolutely right. We are going to fight. This is not how our story ends. Not even close."

34 AGENT HOLT

WHEN THE LOCAL jurisdiction arrives to deal with Connor Wheeler's – aka Craig Martin's – body, I'm happy to see Deputy Sheriff Robert Howie. We worked together on a case a few months back. "Hey," I say, offering him my hand. "Good to see you."

"Look at you, Agent Holt," Howie says. "It's been a while. You doing okay?"

I shrug and look at the dead body behind me on Willow Grace's tiled floor. "I've been better."

"I was surprised when I got this call about Willow and her house being broken into. She okay?"

"That's to be determined. My guess is, though, she was abducted."

"Oh, shit," he says, raking a hand over his head. I worked with him side-by-side when we took down the Harmony cult, not far from Willow's home. Howie's a little gruff around the edges, but I think it's mostly because he's a country man through and through.

I feel my phone start to buzz in my pocket. "Hey, give me a sec," I say, and step outside on the front porch. I have a view of the wilderness, and also the dozens of law enforcement vehicles aiding in this new case. The caller ID shows Smith's name. "Hey, what's up? You almost here?"

"Actually, change of plans. I need you to come to Seattle."

"Why? What's going on?"

"So that girl Chelsea you found in the woods, one of the abductees? She's just been kidnapped again. Her dad was shot."

"Shit," I say, needing a moment to gather my thoughts. "All right. I'll be there as soon as I can. The local cops are here, dealing with the situation at Willow's place."

"Sounds good," Smith says. "Hang tight."

I walk back into Willow's home and fill Howie in. "Don't worry about things here," he says. "I'll keep you posted. Just get Willow back home safe." His eyes lock on mine and I know that he understands that my care for Willow extends beyond the present incident. The connection I had with her was obvious, even back then when we first met.

I give him a nod and head back toward Seattle. I feel like all I've been doing lately is crisscrossing this corridor. Part of me wishes Willow didn't live so far out in Olympia, but it's where her job is, and my job keeps me at the agency in downtown Seattle. We're about an hour apart, and sometimes, like right now, it feels like that stretch of highway goes on forever.

I took everything in that manila envelope with me. I put it in my car before the police arrived, not wanting them to know I was leaving with undocumented evidence. Maybe that's not above board, but I don't really care right now. All I care about is making sure Willow gets home safe. I owe her a lot more than that, but it'll be a start.

When I get close to the Seattle exit, I plug in the address that Smith texted me and navigate to the Hammond home. The idea that he's been shot slays me. He was a good man, one who cares deeply for his child.

When I get to the house and park, I'm shocked to see Smith and Leroy talking on the porch, dimly lit by the glowing lanterns around the outer wall. Before, I'd assumed Leroy had been murdered.

I park my car and jog up to them. "I thought you were going to be at the hospital," I say to Leroy.

"It was just a shot to the arm," he says. "It blew me down pretty hard. Feel like a damn wuss because if I had been stronger, I could have gone after her."

"Right, "I say. "Because you were going to go after two armed men who were holding your daughter against her will?"

He sighed and looked down at his wounded arm. "I know," he says.

"That probably would've been a stupid idea. She could have been the one who ended up getting hurt."

"Exactly. So don't talk like that," I tell him. "You get bandaged up pretty good?"

Smith answered for him, "Yeah. He refused to let anyone put him in an ambulance. He said, 'Wrap me up here because I got to go find my girl.'"

My eyebrows raised, impressed. "All right," I say. "So. You're more than an Army Ranger. You're a goddamn fighter, huh?"

"Hell yeah, I am! So where do you think they are?" he asks.

I look over at Smith. "What's happening? We're looping Leroy in now?"

"Here's the thing, boss," Smith begins. "I know you think Willow's been pulled back into her cult. Wherever she came from and wherever that cult is--"

I cut him off. "I have information. I've got a map."

"So you got some map, but like, I can't exactly get a search warrant for some cult in the middle of nowhere without hard evidence that they're connected in any way to what's going on."

"But there is evidence. There's the file that was found about Willow's history. They went after her. Why else would she be connected to the situation with the girls who were kidnapped?"

"I don't know," Smith says. "But after Waco, I can't exactly bring in a SWAT team without proof that they're connected at all."

"Fine," I say, beginning to pace the porch now. "It's all bullshit."

"What?" Smith says. "You think you can get the FBI to show up there and blow the place up?"

"I know it's not that simple," I say. "But hell, I wish it were easier."

"So what's your plan?" Smith asks me.

"My plan is to go get Willow and Chelsea."

"What I don't understand," Leroy says, "is why they would want Chelsea. I mean, hell, if Willow escaped from this cult years ago, I can understand why they want *her*. But what does Chelsea have to do with anything? What do five thirteen-year-old girls have to do with this place, Fountain of Fellowship?"

"Fountain of Faith," I tell him. "That's the name of it. Ring a bell?"

Both Smith and Leroy shake their heads. "Never heard of the place."

"It's on the coast, north of Aberdeen."

"All right," Leroy says.

"We should go." I look at Smith, then Leroy.

"What?" Smith asks. "You want me to come along?"

"I want you to do whatever you want to do."

Smith grins. "I already told you. This is my last case. Might as well go out with a bang. Come on, boys, let's go make a scene!"

35 WILLOW

SOME MOMENTS in life are so profound that you know they will be a part of your story forever, these isolated incidents that define who you are, who you've been, who you're going to be.

That's how I feel when the van comes to a stop, and the back door opens, letting the light flood in. At that moment, I'm still bound, ankles and wrists, as is Chelsea. And I hope, in this small part of me, that I can stay tucked against myself forever, in a tight ball, avoiding everything that lay outside of that van.

It isn't an option, though. The man tells us to come forward.

"It's a little difficult," I say, "considering we're tied up."

They grab our ankles and drag us forward, cutting the ropes, setting our feet free. They each pull out a gun. "If you want to run, you can."

"You're not going to shoot me," I say, my voice taut with years of pent-up anger. "Father Flint doesn't want me dead."

"You don't know what he wants."

"Maybe I do," I say. "I don't know who you are, but I used to be married to your prophet. I know he wants me alive."

I feel Chelsea staring at me. And I wish I could console her, tell her that everything's going to be okay, but I can't. I don't know what they have planned for us. All I know is we're being led, side by side, to a compound that's so familiar to me, it makes my skin crawl, my bones brittle, my heart ache. I've been trying to avoid this place for so long.

Why did I stay in Washington? Why didn't I take a Greyhound bus across the country, go as far away as possible, to Boston or Atlanta, Vermont? Why did I, instead, choose to stay so close to home? I've only been two hours from this place, all this time.

In truth, I do know why. Because Bethany is still here. My mother was buried here. I hoped they would one day forgive me for leaving and for not coming back. I always hoped I would eventually get the courage to be brave enough to fight for their freedom, for their mercy, too. Yet somehow, fifteen years had passed, and I still hadn't made it back here.

Until now, that is. But this isn't how I'd imagined returning.

So maybe I've been fooling myself all along. Maybe I was never coming back of my own free will, not for them. And so maybe the love I have for them hasn't been as true as I wanted to believe it was. But I also know it's why I haven't made women friends in my new life, why the chatter of the women at the hair salon was so foreign to me and something I hadn't allowed myself to have since I had moved away from Fountains of Freedom. It felt like a betrayal to the women I did love. The women I left behind.

I'm thinking all these things as we're led to a house I know all too well. A house that used to be my home. But instead of going through the main entrance, we're led around the back.

"Where's everybody else?" Chelsea asks.

Our captors look back at us. "It's not your job to ask questions."

But there is an eerie sense of calm settling across the compound. There are only three main buildings that house people. It's an apartment-style complex that Flint bought years ago, back in the '70s. It has twenty units, and that's where everyone except for him lives. He built this house for himself, later. And then there's the church.

I'd explain this to Chelsea, but not in front of these men. I don't want them to know how well I know the lay of this land.

Behind the house is a door that leads to the basement, and that's where they take us.

"There's no way out," they tell us, as we get to the bottom of the stairs. "Sit here until we come back for you."

They walk back up the stairs, guns still pointed at us, and I watch them leave. As soon as the door is bolted shut and locked – a thick, metal door at that – I turn around and see three other girls sitting on blankets on the concrete floor.

"Oh my God," I say. "Are you the other girls who were kidnapped last week?"

"I'm Rachel," one of them says.

"I'm Tori."

"I'm Brittany."

"I'm Willow," I tell them, sitting down on the floor in front of them. Chelsea does too. Their hands are tied, same as mine. "Have you tried to get out?"

Tori speaks up. "We've tried everything. It's no use. We're going to hurt ourselves if we do anymore." She shows me her arm. It's all black and blue. "I threw myself against that metal door so many times. It won't budge. The windows all have metal grates."

"I broke that one," Rachel says, pointing to a window above a washing machine. "But all I did was cut my hand." She shows me the dried blood crusted around the knuckles on her hand.

"They bring us food, though," Brittany says. "A couple times a day, and it's actually good."

"We don't need to compliment them," Tori shoots back.

"I'm not complimenting them," Brittany says. "I'm just saying the food's actually good. We had like this lentil soup and—"

"Stop it," Tori says. "You're making it sound like they're the good guys."

"No, I'm not. I'm just saying."

"Let's not fight," Chelsea says. "Please, let's not fight."

"Where's Ruby?" Brittany asks.

Chelsea blinks, her eyes once again filled with tears. "She died." The girls are stunned. Silent. "They were chasing us in the woods, and I jumped in the river, and Ruby tried to. But then she died. She fell on the shore and ... "

"You got away?" Tori asks her.

Chelsea nodded. "For a few days. I was going to die out there in the woods from hypothermia, or a coyote was going to kill me, and then, some-how, I was found. They helicoptered me out, and I was at a hospital, but they came to my dad's house, once I got home. They shot him, and they shoved me back in the van."

The girls sat in stunned silence for a moment. I wanted so badly to take all of them in a tight, comforting hug.

"Why us?" Rachel asks. "Why us, out of anybody?"

I listened to the girls, but I wonder if they notice what I see. The resemblance between all of us is surprising.

"We all kind of look the same." Tori says. "We have the same dark hair, you know? Dark eyes. Just like you," she says, looking at me. Then she tilts her head, wearing a curious expression. "Why'd they come get you?"

Chelsea pipes in, her voice clear. She's a fighter, in ways I didn't realize in the van when she was crying. She's strong. She's tough. I like her.

"She used to live here. She was married to the guy in charge. It's like a cult, like a freaky cult."

"Seriously?" Brittany asks. "We were kidnapped by a cult? What are they going to do, like, sacrifice us?"

"I don't think so," I say. "It's not that kind. It's a religious cult, more than anything."

"Don't religious people do sacrifices, like human sacrifices?" Rachel says. "Oh God, are they going to eat us alive?"

"Nobody is going to be cannibalized," Chelsea says. "We can't get hysterical. We have to stay smart."

Just then, the door opens.

"Oh, God," Brittany starts to cry. "They're going to eat us now, aren't they?"

"Stop it," Chelsea hisses.

"Listen," I say. "Just stay quiet. It'll be the best thing if you want to get out of here alive."

Our eyes lock, and then a man reaches the end of the stairs. He's flanked by two others, the men who kidnapped us. They're the ones holding the guns.

The man in the center, though, is a man I know. More intimately than I wish I did.

"You've returned to the fold," he says, speaking to me. A wide grin stretches across his wrinkling features. He's certainly aged in the last fifteen years.

"I didn't return. I was taken."

"Stand up."

When I refuse, his voice gets loud. "Stand up. Now," he says.

The men with the guns take a step toward me, so I do as he asks.

"What do you want with me?"

"You are the prophecy fulfilled."

"You are not a real prophet," I say. "You are nothing but a fool."

"I'm your husband."

"I was a child."

"You still are my wife."

"I'm nothing to you."

"You're everything to the congregation."

"Don't say that," I say. I'm tempted to spit at him, but I know that wouldn't end in my favor. Or the girls'. "Why'd you put me in this wedding dress? You're going to marry me all over again?"

"Yes," he says. "I am, in a special ceremony."

"And the girls, why are they here? Why would you bring them into your disaster, into this sick, twisted fantasy you've made all of these people believe?"

"Because, my bride, can't you see?"

"See what?" I ask, looking back at the girls.

"They are our children. The ones we never had."

Horror and disgust fill my insides. "These girls, you kidnapped them... to be their father?"

"And you will be their mother." He approaches me and places his hands on my shoulders. I try not to squirm beneath his too-firm grasp. "Don't you see? It was written in our book, all those years ago, that you would bear me five children, five daughters."

"There's only four here," Chelsea says. "How's that prophecy going to work? What are the people in your cult going to think when you only have four girls instead of five?"

Father Flint's eyes narrow. "We're going to have to tame *you*, aren't we?"

"Don't speak to her like that," I say.

He removes his hand from my shoulder and slaps me hard across the cheek. It burns with a fury, but I refuse to cry. I refuse to wince. I clench my jaw.

"We'll find a fifth. We'll just amend the prophecy and say, 'The fifth child is a baby girl, that will come to us in due time.'"

He smiles, his breath like sour milk. My stomach coils in disgust.

"I hate you."

He grins. "You love me." He lets out a sigh, filling my nostrils with the unpleasant odor. "It's time," he tells them the men. "Gather the girls."

"It's time for what?" I ask.

"For our new vows, the vows we'll all make as a family. But first, we need to get our daughters cleaned up, don't you think? They can't go to our ceremony dressed like that. They need to be dressed in white, pure as doves. Just like you. My perfect wife."

36 HOLT

WHEN WE ARRIVE at the location on Willow's hand-drawn maps, I'm surprised to see there's no security system in place. "Seems strange, right?" I say to Leroy and Smith. They both agree with shrugs and nods.

We're all in my car. Smith has outfitted us each with a radio to stay in touch. And before we left Leroy's house, he gave us bulletproof vests. I have one of my own, but the fact that this dude had a whole closet full of gear impressed me.

I watched as he put a gun on his hip, but made no comments. Smith and I are carrying too. And after all, we're here to get the girls and Willow out in one piece. That might mean the bad guys have to lose.

"Maybe it's not about a security system," Smith says, "but keeping people in line. It's about their beliefs. They don't need barbed wire fences. Whoever's in charge would use psychological control and I bet they have plenty of it. From what I read in Willow's paperwork, they sure had a hold on her."

During our drive to the coast, he's been reading the documents in the folder. Both he and Leroy had whistled low several times as they read aloud Willow's documents. How most of the members of the congregation were women, single moms with no money, no food, no shelter. They were lured in out of desperation.

The men who lived here loved control and power, and they found it by forcing these women to be their wives. It makes me sick the way people abuse others, but right now, I can't focus on the indoctrination of this place. Right now, I need to focus on where I can park this car, so I don't raise any red flags.

"I'm just going to pull into the woods here and then we'll hike in. Sound good?" Leroy and Smith agree.

We lock the vehicle and begin walking toward the compound, discussing the lay of the land and using Willow's maps as guides. It looks like there are three buildings. "That one, that big apartment complex must be where everyone lives. I'm guessing that's where the leader lives," Smith says, pointing to a big farmhouse. "And that must be the church. There's a big old cross in the front."

"What a creepy place to grow up," Leroy says. "Can you imagine?"

"I can't," I say. And even though I grew up with a mom who was an addict, struggling to make ends meet, I'm sure glad we never ended up at a place like this, a place that would've made my future so small.

"I think we should split up," Leroy says. "This way, we can each do our best to locate the girls."

"Yeah, I agree," I say. "As soon as someone finds them, we can call in the calvary." Until I've got proof that they're here, I'm operating off the reservation and willing to do anything I need to to save everyone, no matter the cost.

"I'm going to head around the house," Leroy says.

I watch him go, and I head toward the church. Smith goes to the complex. I have my eye on Leroy, surprised at his willingness to jump all in, knowing what's at stake, his actual life – but he has a daughter to rescue.

I don't into anyone as I walk around the perimeter of the church. I reach the back of the building the same time Leroy gets to the back of the farmhouse. I watch as he comes across a guard standing at the back door of the house.

"Who are you?" the man asks Leroy.

I want to radio something, but I'm going to stay quiet. I walk toward them, keeping my distance, but close enough to serve as a backup if necessary. I watch as Leroy answers with a swift elbow to the head, knocking the man to the ground. A moment later Leroy kneels on him, his knee deep in his chest, silently choking him out.

I watch in shock and surprise, but also in understanding. Hell, Leroy had his daughter taken by this group twice. He's going to do whatever he can to get her back. And I can't blame him for using violence against anyone who might have taken her.

Now with the coast clear, I get a radio call from him. "The house is empty, at least the back of it. Where are you guys?"

"Same here at the church. No one's out. I think everyone's inside this building."

"Makes sense," Smith says. "The apartment's empty too."

The three of us join together behind the complex. We're looking for any proof that we're right about the connection because otherwise, we're going to have to leave fast and regroup.

"Look," I say. "Through that window." Everyone really is in the church. We're hunkered beneath the window, observing the interior of the commune. I scan the premises, and spot the white van parked behind a stable.

I pull out my binoculars. It's our van. "Look, there's a blue paint transfer on the fender," I say, handing the binoculars to Smith. I pull out my phone wanting to relay the information to Tamara.

"Dammit," I say. "No reception."

"You'd have to get to higher ground and risk exposure," Leroy says. "I think we should go at it alone."

I look at him. And with these two strong men at my side, I believe we have the power to do it. "Use your binoculars and see if you can identify Willow and Chelsea and the other girls," Smith says.

I zoom in at the window of the church. I see dozens of people inside. "I don't see them," I say. "But the view's not great."

"I'll go closer," Smith says, taking the binoculars from me. He steps forward. Leroy and I both pull out our guns, in case Smith needs backup since he's the one crossing the grounds toward the church.

He kneels in front of a window and begins scanning. A few minutes later, he returns. It's eerie how quiet everything is outside.

"What do you think? See anything?" I ask him.

"Nothing. I don't think they're there, but everybody else is. Bunch of women, bunch of kids, way less men. Sickos," Leroy says, shaking his head.

I couldn't agree more. "Smith, you're sure no one's in the apartment building?"

Smith nods. "No one's in there. And get this, all the doors were unlocked. I bet these people don't even have keys. "

"It's like a ghost town except they're all in the church, minus the people we're looking for," I say. "That means they're in the house."

"Let's go," Smith says.

When we get to the front door though, we're spotted. Dammit. Two men. "These are the guys who came to my house," Leroy says. "Pieces of shit. The one bandaged up pretty bad, my girl did that," he tells me. His face fills with pride. And smugness. "Hit that bastard with a tire iron."

I smirk despite everything. Leroy raised a good one, and knowing how tough he is, I'm not surprised.

"This won't end well for you," one of the men says to us. "You're on our property now."

Another man comes out of the front door, joining us. He's older and he's wearing a suit and tie. Immediately, I want to kill him. This must be the man who'd held Willow captive all those years The prophet, Father Flint. As he begins to speak, his gravelly voice makes me sick. "I demand you leave our premises before we're forced to take action. You're on private property without a proper warrant."

"There's three of us," Leroy says. "I'm not leaving here without my daughter, you try to stop me."

"We have more backup," Flint says. "I have plenty of men ready to fight on my behalf – the Lord's behalf, rather." He leaves, anger flashing in his eyes.

But Leroy is filled with rage. He's locked eyes on the man I've never seen before, but who I'm guessing is the one who'd attacked him at his house. "You already shot me once," Leroy spits at the man. "I'm not going to let you get away now." He launches at the man and chaos erupts.

Leroy has his gun pointed at his target.

"Stop. You don't need to," Smith says.

Leroy doesn't see that the man has a gun too. He's so charged with anger that he doesn't realize he's putting himself at risk. Not wanting either of them to die, I shoot the man coming for Leroy. I hit him in the leg. The last thing I'm going to do is kill a guy and deal with more bullshit moving forward, but I will do what it takes to knock him out.

Leroy's target drops to the ground and shouts out in pain from the bullet, red oozing from his leg. Leroy launches at the man with the bandaged head. They start rolling around on the ground.

"I'm going to kill you," Leroy says, the look in his eyes tells me he is out for blood. His little girl means everything to him. He won't back down from making someone pay. "I'm goings to kill you for what you did to my daughter."

"What she did to me!" The man fights back. They have hands at one another's necks. Someone's going to die, but I see the fury in Leroy, and I know it's not going to be him. "You're going to pay for what you did. You take those girls and you think you own them? You're wrong."

The man on the ground is gasping for breath, his grip loosening from Leroy's throat. Leroy stands, his foot on the man's chest, and he shoots him straight in the heart. Shit.

That's the last thing I wanted to see happen, but Leroy came here on a mission. He was looking for vengeance and it looks like he's getting some.

37 WILLOW

WE'VE BEEN BROUGHT into my old home. The fact that I'm in here at all makes me feel sick to my stomach. It has been fifteen years and it smells the same, looks the same, feels the same. Nothing has changed. The pine scent of the floor wax and the orange scented wood polish. There are doilies on the arms of the furniture, ones I know I made myself.

Flint moved us to a side bedroom that he always said would be a nursery. There is still a crib in it, a rocking chair. I feel ill. This man will never have a child of his own. And God help me, the girls at my side will never be his daughters.

In the nursery, it's not just the furniture that causes me to gasp. It's Bethany. Her eyes lock with mine and her eyes fill with tears. The shame that washes over me is untenable.

"You remember Sister Bethany?" Flint says to me with a smirk, knowing I would never forget my dearest friend.

"Of course I do," I manage to say, fighting the emotion gathering in my throat.

The armed men have followed us in the room as well and now there is a third, a man I know. Bethany's husband Thomas.

"Bethany is here to prepare you all for the ceremony. Thomas, you'll stand at the door. Understood?"

Flint and the other two men exit the room.

Thomas pauses and looks at me. "It's been a long time."

I swallow, unable to gather a response. Bethany, Thomas, and I were friends when we were young. Now he looks so old. Bethany looks just the same. Blue-eyed and pink-cheeked as ever.

Thomas leaves the room, closing the door.

Bethany and I stare at one another for a long moment.

"Bethany," I say. "It's been so long it's..."

"Don't," she says. She walks around the room pulling items out of drawers. Items I remember from my first wedding. "Don't apologize. You shouldn't have come back."

"I wasn't trying to come back. He forced me to. You should hate me."

She stops in her tracks and looks at me, sympathy flooding her expression. "Why would I hate you?" She rushes toward me, wrapping her arms around me. It's a hug I've been wanting for fifteen years and I wrap my arms around her right back. For so long, this is the kind of connection I've pulled away from. Been too scared to have. My eyes begin stinging with tears. I don't try to fight it.

The girls with me watch in confusion as the scene unfolds.

"I'm so sorry. I wanted to call the police or tell someone, but I didn't want any harm to come to you or anyone else, especially not your children."

"I know," she said. "I never thought you would say something. I just wish you had told me you were leaving."

"How could I? I didn't want you to be in any trouble. I just didn't think after this long he would still care enough to pull me back."

She lets go of me and begins picking out accessories again. "He had a prophecy recently."

"No," I say. "What happened was he saw me in the news. He was able to track me down."

Bethany's eyes search mine. "No, Father would never do that. It's his will. It's..."

My face falls as I realize she is still so brainwashed. She is so wrapped up in the indoctrination at Fountain of Faith that she doesn't realize that she is just a player in Flint's game. A game that he is going to lose. Soon.

"The girls must get dressed," Bethany says. "The ceremony is soon."

"We're not doing that," Chelsea says. "We're not going to some creepy ceremony and letting some guy think he's going to like become our daddy. I already have a dad."

Bethany's eyes widen, but she remains composed. "The prophet said it would be hard for the girls to understand. That it would be a lot of change for them."

"No," I say. "That's not what's happening here."

"Damn right it's not," Tori says. "We already have families and we're going back to them. I don't know what creepy cult you are in, lady, but we're not joining."

"We need to go," I say.

"No," Bethany says. "You've been brought here for the ceremony. For the..."

"No, we're not!" I exclaim. "Are you going to stop me?" I ask her.

"I've missed you so much," she says, her chin quivering as tears fill her eyes once more. "Don't go when you just came back. You're my best friend since forever and..."

"If you love me, you're going to let me go."

"Thomas won't let you go," she answers. "It's his duty to keep you here. "She stares at me for another long moment. I can see in her eyes she doesn't want to be here either. But she's too far gone.

"I need you to put on these dresses," she tells the girls, pointing at the four gowns that are hanging over the wooden rails of the baby crib. "You need to get dressed for the ceremony. It's starting soon."

"No," I say. "They're not putting those things on. They're not playing a part in a game. Not this one. Not this time."

I push open the door of the nursery and outside I hear a gunshot.

"We have to go," Chelsea says. "Now."

Thomas comes in and looks at me. He has a gun in his hand.

"Are you going to shoot me?" I ask him.

But before he even considers it, Chelsea and Tori barrel after him, shoving him down at his waist, catching him off guard. Chelsea kicks the gun out of his hand, picks it up, and gives it to me.

"Do you know how to get out of here?"

I grin. "Yes," I say.

With the gun in my hand, I point it at Thomas. "I won't shoot, but please do not follow."

Bethany covers her mouth and lets out a muffled scream, her eyes wide.

The girls and I rush through the house to the kitchen and out the back door.

"We've got to go to the woods," I say. The five of us have one gun, but five beating hearts. And we are sure as hell not going to stick around to see what happens next.

38 AGENT HOLT

THE GUNSHOTS HAVE CREATED CHAOS. The churchgoers are suddenly flying out the front doors, scared and wanting answers to the questions swirling around. All the men, women and children, are watching, looking for an explanation. I'm guessing that while this cult runs on power and control, the people who live here are not used to being around guns and this level of violence. People are screaming, shouting. Someone's rushing toward the man Leroy just killed.

"Who did this to my husband?"

"Papa! Papa!" Children scream.

I look at Flint, his eyes are wide, his arms lifted in the air. "All is well, my family. All is well. As I've said, before the calm, there will always be a storm." But no one is listening.

Everyone is demanding answers. "Who killed him? Who killed him?" The woman says, kneeling by her deceased husband.

I look at Smith. We know we need to contain the members before this becomes more out of hand. If they start scattering before the cavalry arrives, it's going to be more difficult to determine who was involved and how.

Out of the corner of my eye though, I see Willow and all four of the girls. "Smith, Leroy." Their eyes follow mine. The people who just exited the church are watching my every move, and I realize it's because we are the only outsiders. We are the people they're angry at. We are the killers, and they know it. Willow doesn't step forward. She speaks to the girls, all of them in a huddle and while she stays back, I watch as the four girls rush toward us. With our focus on the girls finally in our custody, I lose sight of Flint.

"Where'd he go?" I ask Smith.

"I don't know. I was focused on Willow."

Leroy wraps his arms around his daughter. "Dad," she cries. "Oh my God, I'm so scared."

"We've got to find Flint. We can't leave the scene," Smith says. "These people are going to get in their cars. They're going to start running. Who the hell knows what's going to happen?"

Willow turns and looks at me, and though she's several yards away, I know what she's saying. She points toward the woods, and she bolts like a cannon. I know what she's doing. She's going after Flint.

I can feel her motivation, I can sense her growing strength. It's as if she has been building up to this moment her whole life.

"Are you going to follow?" Smith asks.

I shake my head. "No. We got to keep these people here. These girls are my priority right now. This was my assignment." I clear my throat and turn to address the commune. "Everyone, I'm Federal Agent Holt. This is Seattle Police Department Investigator Detective Smith. We are here to keep order."

This manages to quiet the crowd and gather their attention, but someone screams, "You're here to kill us!"

The other man who'd held us at gunpoint has dropped his gun. Out the front door walks a couple, a man and a woman, and he lifts his arms up. "I already gave my gun to Willow."

"You don't have more? You're laying down your arms?" I ask them both.

They nod. "I joined this church because I believe in love, not war," Thomas says, his arms wrapping around the woman at his side. "I'm not here to shoot anybody. I never wanted to hold a gun at all."

I look at Smith. "In that case, maybe everyone should return to the church until we can detain your prophet."

39 WILLOW

Of course Flint fled, leaving his congregation the moment he realized an FBI agent was here and there was no getting out of this. He's always been a coward, a fool. What's always been the most shocking to me is that people believe him. People like Bethany who, even when faced with the truth, choose to turn a blind eye. That's why it's so hard for anyone to leave a place like this, because when you have built your entire life around an ideology, the idea of it being false would shatter who you are at your very core.

But now I have the chance to take the situation into my own hands. Flint has a head start. I'll give him that, but there's no way in hell this man is winning. I may not have been here in fifteen years, but I still know these woods. It's where I grew up. It's where I spent my childhood. It's where Bethany and I would climb a tree and sit and talk about what our future would be like, getting married and having children, all under the assumption that it would be happening here, of course, in the Fountain of Faith.

But never did I think I would be marrying the prophet. I remember when he first told the church that I was to be his bride. Bethany took my hand and clasped it. She was so happy for me. It was an honor, but I didn't love him. I had never been in love. I wasn't even attracted to him. And the idea that I was going to married to that man, a man at least twice my age? We'd never even spoken one-on-one. I'd always wondered why he picked me. But he had a choice to make, and he'd made it. He wanted me to be his. And he called it God's Will. It was hard to argue with that.

My mother, of course, had been dead for years by then. She died only three years after we moved here. Cancer, I'm sure. But no one would take her to the hospital. No one would give her treatment. She died because she was never given proper care. I always guessed it was lung cancer. Growing up, she smoked at least a pack a day, and in the end, she would cough so much until there was nothing but blood in the tissue that she pressed to her mouth. So, then I was alone and Bethany was my friend and her family took me in as a part of theirs.

Everyone was so honored. The prophet said I was an orphan and now I would be a part of the Father's family. Even then, I think it was just a story he'd spun to make himself sound better. What choice did I have but to follow? I was not the girl I am now. Now I'm strong. I escaped. I understand what kind of monster he is that preys on young people, young women, young children, people who are vulnerable, men who are desperate, who want to feel some sort of power in their lives, and they find it here. But it's time to end this part of my life. This chapter needs to come to a close.

"What do you think you're going to do?" Flint says, turning to me when I catch up to him. He's gasping for air.

"I'm going to kill you," I say plainly, holding the gun up, walking toward him.

It's dark now. The weather has turned cold and I feel drops of rain on my shoulder. We haven't had any showers for days on end, but now of course, they come to wipe away the past with more than a metaphor.

"You won't kill me," he says, "You love me."

"I've never loved you."

"Yes, you did," he says, "I remember how you and I used to make love."

"It was never love," I say. "You forced me. I was a child."

"No, you were my wife," he says in a loud growl.

I feel sick. Nauseous at the memories, memories I've repressed. And even though I went to therapy for plenty of years, these are stories I could never say out loud. Put words to. Flint sees the look in my eye. The fury and rage burning inside me. He must, because he backs up.

"Oh, you're going to run now?" I ask him.

His foot catches on a root in the ground and he falls backwards. The scene is so ridiculous, so anti-climactic. The man I hate on his back, looking up at me. I'm holding a gun on him, and still he thinks he's in charge. He thinks he's in control.

"You're not going to do it," he says. "You're going to let down all those people back there. Those women and children and men who have hung their life on the truth of this place, you're going to dismantle everything they believe because you want some power trip right now? Don't be ridiculous. You would never hurt them."

"It's not about hurting them. It's about setting them free."

I raise the gun, and I point it down at the man who forever changed the course of my life.

I'm not going to let his mental gymnastics get me off track. Not now, not ever again.

The gun though, quivers in my hand. I haven't actually killed a person. And I wonder, is he right? Can I do this thing? Can I kill this man? It goes against my very nature. Do I want to be a killer, a murderer? It's not as if Flint is actually threatening me in this moment, but it'll be too difficult to try and use this gun to force Flint back to hold in the others, to try to get him to go with me.

Flint would never budge. He never has.

And in my hesitation, he reaches for my ankle.

He pulls me down to the ground.

"Don't," I say. "Don't touch me."

But as I fall next to him, he rolls on top of me. His confidence growing, making me more than angry, making me furious. He laughs, looking down at me, thinking he's got me, but he's wrong. I still have the gun. And even though it's not going to be a clean shot with my arm pinned down, I still hold the gun in my fingers and I move my wrist, tilting it up.

I pull the trigger and the gun erupts.

I'm not sure where the bullet's going to land, but the fact that it hits his skull sends a sense of power over me I've never felt before.

Then in the next instant, I'm showered with his blood as he drops on top of me. The weight of this man is a memory so vile I scream with a fury I've never expressed in my life. I shove him off of me with all of my power, all of my might.

It is me holding the gun as I stand, looking down at his body. I'm covered in his blood. His head has a bullet in it. He's dead. I have an urge to use every bullet in this gun to obliterate the rest of his body, but I don't. I can't. I'm not going to make this messier than it already is. I've killed the leader who has forced me to spend countless years looking over my shoulder. That was my aim.

I realize I am the lucky one. Not because I'm covered in his blood, but because people like Linda Benedict, who I'd met with earlier this week, never had this actual sense of release, this complete understanding that she had her life back.

But I do. And no one will ever take it from me again.

Trembling with a confidence I've never felt before, I walk out of the woods.

When I reach the compound I am shaking, but calm and I make eye contact with Holt.

I hand him the gun.

"Willow," he says.

The relief in his worried eyes tells me everything. He looks at me, the blood across my face, my chest, my hands. It tells him everything he needs to know. He sees me in a way no one else ever has.

He takes my hand in his and squeezes it. I wish he was wrapping me up in a hug, but not now. Not yet, because the calvary has finally arrived. A SWAT team is here, the FBI at their heels.

"We have to clean this mess up first," he says, before adding, "then we'll clean you up. I promise."

40 WILLOW

Once the FBI team arrives, Holt is pulled away to do his job. I watch him go, feeling a sense of relief that he is here, at the compound with me. I don't know where he and I stand exactly, but I do know I'd rather stand by him than be on my own.

An emergency responder comes over to me and offers supplies to help me clean myself up.

"Thank you," I say, taking the towels from them. Wiping my face and hands is strange, knowing that what I am washing away is the blood of the man who'd had so much control of my life for so long. I don't know what's going to happen when they pull me into questioning, when they find his body in the woods, when I have to sit down and tell the entirety of my story, the beginning, the messy middle, and the end. But I know I will have a braver face than I've ever had before. That weight I've been carrying, the shadow that's been following me everywhere, is gone. The rain is just a drizzle and I'm thankful for that. But in this moment, there would be something beautiful about a heavy rain shower, washing all of this away.

I see Chelsea with the man I assume is her father, and I walk over to them. They're sitting on the porch of my old house. "Hey," I say. "Are you doing okay?"

Her dad introduces himself as Leroy.

"I'm Willow Grace," I say. "I met your daughter earlier today in the van."

"She was just telling me about that," Leroy says. "Sounds like you were her guardian angel. The guardian angel for all those girls."

"I don't know about that," I say. "I don't think I was saving anybody. I was just trying to get us out in one piece." Chelsea looks at me as if there's a whole bunch she's ready to say. "What are you thinking?" I ask her.

"I'm thinking you're amazing," she says, blurting it out. "You were so strong in the van. I was just a mess. Dad, I was completely falling apart. I was crying and scared, and Willow was just strong and brave and--"

"Hey, Chelsea," I say. "You were brave. You are the strongest girl I've ever met, and I know your future's bright."

"Yeah?" she asks, tucking a strand of hair behind her ear. "You think so?"

"I know so. You were talking in the van about your feelings about Ruby, about her dying."

"Yeah. How it's my fault?"

"I know you said that before, but I want to remind you, Chelsea, your instinct to fight and survive kicked in. And that doesn't mean you did anything wrong. It means you were willing to do whatever it took to make sure the life that you lived was one that counted. You weren't going to sit back in that van and let someone take it away from you."

"Kind of like you, huh? When you escaped this place all those years ago?

"Maybe."

"I'm going to grow up and be like you, Willow."

Leroy looks at me. "My daughter doesn't usually compliment people that readily."

"It's flattering to hear that, Chelsea. But don't grow up and be like me. Grow up and be like you. The best version of you." She stands and I give her a big hug. "I'm so glad you and your dad are back together."

She smiles at me when she pulls away. "Me too. And just so you know, my dad's single."

Leroy chuckles, "Chelsea. We're not doing that."

I laugh. "Well, that is quite a compliment," I say to Chelsea. "It was great to meet you, Leroy. And I heard you were pretty awesome earlier. I think if you wouldn't have taken that man down, the girls and I would've never had a chance to escape the house. It all worked out."

"Yeah. I guess both you and I had a pretty heavy day, huh?" Leroy asks.

I know what he's referring to.

We both killed a man.

I exhale, a weight lifted. "I guess sometimes you got to do what you got to do."

We exchange unsaid words with our eyes before I walk away feeling at peace. Grateful that Chelsea has a father like she does, the same way I'm grateful that Megan Talbot has her aunt. Everybody needs somebody.

That thought makes me wonder who I have.

I scan the compound and see Holt and Smith talking to a group of other officers. I feel safer knowing he's close. Holt always seems to have my back.

Bethany walks over to me and I'm surprised to see a smile on her face considering everything that's happened here today. "I wanted to talk to you before you left," she said.

"I wasn't rushing away," I tell her.

"I know. Just, I want you to know I love you, and I never held it against you that you didn't come back for me. Truth is, Willow, I wouldn't have left. By the time you were trying to go, Tom and I were already in love. I already had a baby, a second one on the way. I was never going to leave here."

"And now?" I ask.

Bethany says, "Now, I don't think I have a choice. Tom has some family in Oregon. We might head down there. I have five girls now."

"Wow," I say.

She turns and points to a group of children, but there are so many of them.

"Can you believe that Ruth Anne is almost eighteen years old?"

I shake my head. I really can't. The math makes sense, though. Bethany's 35 now and she had Ruth Anne when she was just seventeen. "Time goes by so fast," I say, not knowing what other words to use. What else might sound true. Bethany and I made such different life choices. The divide is so big. And even though I've always held such a tender spot in my heart for her, I realize now, standing before her, that there's a lifetime between us.

"I was wondering," she said, "Would you want to keep in touch?"

I smile. "I would love nothing more," I tell her.

She doesn't have a phone. So we walk into my old house, Flint's farmhouse, and head to the kitchen to find a piece of paper and a pen.

"Is it weird to be back in here?" she asks.

I nod. "So weird. I spent so long trying to forget this place and now that I'm here, there are so any memories."

"Remember that summer we pickled all those cucumbers in here, but then we used the wrong ratio of vinegar, and they all went bad?"

I laugh. "We were just kids."

"Sixteen years old," she says. "I was barefoot and pregnant in this kitchen, and you were just thanking your lucky stars that you weren't."

"Yeah. But you were in love with Tom," I say. "It was different for you. Flint and I, we were never..."

Bethany pauses. "Did you really shoot him, out in the woods?"

I press my lips together, meeting her eyes. Her blonde hair has gray in it. There are wrinkles around her eyes, but gosh, she's just as lovely as I remember. "I did. But he would've killed me if I didn't kill him."

She nods. "That's probably true. You don't think he was ever a prophet?"

"I think you already know what I think."

She swallows. "Do you think I'm a fool for staying all this time?"

I shake my head. "No. I don't think you're a fool. I think you made choices that were right for you, for your family, and everybody makes choices that are different. And it's not my place to judge yours. Same way as it's not your place to judge mine."

She nods, taking a deep breath. "What did you do when you left?" she asks me.

"I put one foot in front of the other for a long, long time. And Bethany, you're going to do the same thing and your life is going to be big. It's going to be beautiful, and in a lot of ways, it's only just begun."

Tears are in her eyes and she wraps her arms around me, giving me another hug. "I've never had a friend like you. Not since you left," she tells me. "It's like there was a you-shaped hole in my heart."

Her words are like a balm I didn't know I needed. The truth in them hits home. I have been feeling the same exact way.

"On that note," she says, "Give me your number. We can get together sometime. You can tell me all about your life." Then she asks, "So you never married, never had any kids?"

I shake my head. "Nope. Never."

"Any regrets?" she asks.

"Yes," I say. "We all have regrets. I think people are lying if they say they don't."

"What kind of regrets do you have?" Bethany asks me, cutting straight to the heart of things.

"I regret that I was scared for so long. I think I did that to myself. Chose to live in the shadows. If I could do it all over again, I would've spent a lot more time in my life being bold."

I write down my phone number on a slip of paper and I hand it to Bethany. "I'm never coming back to this place," I tell her.

"Yeah, I don't think I am either." She twists her lips, taking the paper from me and slipping it into her apron pocket. It is clear she is still in shock, that the reality of her quickly changing life hasn't hit her yet. I hope that when she begins to grasp the enormity of change, she will be facing in the coming months, she has the support she needs to carve out a new way of living.

We walk out the front door together and I look out at the compound. This place that has felt like a noose around my neck for so damn long. Finally the rope has been discarded. Nothing is holding me back.

"What's next for you?" she asks me.

I smile. "That's a crazy thing, Bethany. I feel like I'm free for the first time in my whole life."

"What will you do with all that freedom?" she asks.

I grin. "I have no idea, but I'm sure as hell ready to find out."

41 AGENT HOLT

I AM SITTING at my desk at the agency when Smith walks up to my cubicle. "Hey, want to grab a coffee?"

I grin. "And a donut?"

"Damn, we're such a cliche," Smith says, laughing. I introduce him to my coworker Jedd, and they shake hands.

"Want me to bring you back anything?" I ask him.

"Nah," Jedd says, "I'm headed out soon anyways on another call."

"Nice to meet you," Smith says, then turns to me as we walk out. "He seems like a nice guy."

"Yeah," I say. "He's pretty cool. Hey, have you ever met Tamara? My boss."

He shakes his head. "Nope, haven't yet." We stop in her office and I make the introductions.

Tamara, being the badass bitch that she is, grills him. "So you are retiring early? How old are you?"

"Forty," Smith says.

She crosses her arms, assessing him. "Why are you leaving the force?"

He shrugs. "I think it's mostly that I'm sick of wearing a uniform."

"I thought you were a detective?"

"I have to wear a tie."

"All right," Tamara says slowly. "You're giving up your pension and everything for that?"

"I'm ready to try something different. I'm going to work on my own."

"What does that mean?" she asks. "Are you going to get some telework job or start a blog?"

Smith smiles. "I'm going to open my own private investigation agency."

Tamara twists her lips. "Interesting. Are you saying local?"

"I think so. For now. My wife's headed to Nashville for a bit to work recording an album, so I'll go out there with her for a while, but then I think I'll come back here and work. This is the beat I know."

Tamara presses her lips together. "Interesting."

"How so?" Smith says.

Tamara touches a finger to her chin. "Well, I'm guessing Holt is going to really enjoy having a guy who isn't bound to any jurisdiction when new cases come up for him. Looks like you guys will be spending a lot more time together."

I snort. "You think I'm going to call Smith in for consults?"

Smith laughs. And Tamara gives me a grin, adding, "Well, you called in Willow three times already."

"Okay, enough," I say. "You can't grill Smith anymore, and you're not asking any more questions about Willow."

Tamara lifts her hands in defense. "Fine. I know. That's your business. You can do what you want to do with it."

"It's nice to meet you, Tamara."

Smith and I take an elevator down to the first floor. "She seems like a cool boss."

"She's awesome. She's one of those agents who just knows her shit through and through and takes nothing from nobody. It's why she's so successful."

"And what about you?" Smith laughs. "You take shit from everybody?"

"Probably too much shit. Damn it."

He chuckles. "Is Willow giving you a hard time these days?"

I give him side eye as we walk to the donut shop. "Willow would never give me a hard time."

"Why is that?" Smith asks.

"Because she's just not that kind of person."

Smith isn't having it. "I don't know. She's been through hell. She's tough. I bet she's tough on you."

"Can we not talk about Willow and me?"

Smith elbows me as he orders himself an Americano and an old-fashioned. I ask for a maple bar and a latte, then we sit down at a table.

"So, what's next for you?" I ask. "You going out to Nashville for a bit?"

He nods. "Yeah, we'll be there for Christmas. I think it'll be kind of cool to spend the month of December somewhere else."

"And your wife? She's happy?"

"Thrilled. It's like a whole dream come true."

"And you don't have any regrets about leaving the force?"

"No," he says, shaking his head. "I've been unhappy for a long time. I'm ready to do my own thing, be my own man. And just because I made a choice to be a police officer when I was twenty-four years old doesn't mean that has to be my entire life story."

"That's true. We can always reinvent ourselves."

"What about you, Holt? Are you going to reinvent yourself?"

"At the moment? I don't know." The waitress comes over with our orders and I take a burning sip of the latte before asking, "Did you see the article that Veronica Little wrote?"

Smith shakes his head. We both pull up our phones and he opens The Seattle Times app. " Damn. Look at us. An untouchable group of heroes."

"You really hadn't seen this?" I ask. "Everyone in the office was talking about it this morning."

"I didn't go to the office this morning," Smith tells me. "But that's mostly because I got an email that gave me a slap on the wrist for breaking protocol when I followed you out yesterday."

"What did your boss say?" I ask.

"I guess he's giving me a pass. Not that it really matters, considering I put in my retirement papers. Truth is, I like the idea of going out on a high note like this."

I scan the article once more, along with Smith.

"It's pretty badass," he says. "Veronica really wrote us up like we were hometown heroes."

"Yeah. Well, that woman is always a little bit more complimentary than necessary."

"She have the hots for you?" Smith asks me.

I grimace. "I don't know if it matters."

He grins. "Nice. That means you must really like your new girl."

"I don't know if Willow's my girl yet."

He chortles, "So where are things at with her?"

I shrug, taking a bite of my maple bar. "I want to see if I can bring her into the fold with the FBI."

"Good thinking," Smith laughs. "That way you can keep your girlfriend close."

I smack him on the shoulder, laughing, wondering when the hell I've had a friend like him before and thanking God that I do.

42 WILLOW

WHEN HOLT CALLS and invites me to dinner, I give him shit about it.

"And you're not going to cancel on me at the last minute?"

He gives a long groan. "I swear I'm not."

I laugh. "Is this just because you're in between cases so you're sure nothing's going to call you in?"

He lets out a sigh and says, "I deserve that. But I was thinking... let me make you dinner. You've cooked for me already and I have one really great meal that I do. I'm going to pull out all the stops."

"Oh really? And what is this?"

"It's risotto with a salmon filet, and asparagus on the side."

"Okay, well, that sounds delicious, " I tell him. "When were you thinking?"

"How about tonight?"

It's been a whirlwind the last twenty-four hours, but the truth is I'd love to spend some time with Holt, and even though he was with me at the end of the situation yesterday, we didn't get a chance to talk. Now that I'm well-rested and had a day off from work, I feel energized to see him.

"No pressure. But if you wanted to stay the night so you didn't have to drive back to Olympia, you can. I have an extra bedroom, and I swear it doesn't have to be more than that."

"That's actually a good idea," I say. "It's been a long few days."

"It certainly has," Holt says. "So tonight? Six? Seven?"

"Seven sounds great," I tell him.

"See you then."

I end the phone call and walk to my bedroom feeling a little giddy. Maybe it's the fact that my hair looks great and I picked up a whole bunch of packages from the PO box this morning, all the clothes I ordered online a few days ago.

It's strange being in this house, considering this is where Connor died only yesterday. I'm trying not to think about that too hard, considering his name wasn't even Connor. There had been a split second where I wondered if he was up to something criminal when he'd sent that cryptic message about a relic from his past. But when the medical examiner called this morning to let me know that there was something on his person that I might like to have, I asked what it was.

"It was an envelope," the examiner told me, "with your name on it. Inside was a necklace."

"Anything on the necklace?"

"No, but he had a matching one, so ... "

"He was wearing a matching one?"

"Yes," the examiner says. "And etched on the back, it says, 'We are survivors.'"

The medical examiner told me he'd send it and I thanked him, but I wasn't quite sure if I even wanted the necklace. Connor was not forthright. He'd lied about being a student at Conifer College and he was obviously dedicated to learning everything he could about me. He was stalking me really, and I understand why a survivor might do something like that. He found a connection with me and wanted to establish something more emotional, and he did a very good job of that. If he was still alive, I would tell him that he was actually projecting some of the trauma he faced from his past onto me. Even if Connor was doing that unintentionally, it was still harm that I don't want.

If I think about it too much, it makes me sad knowing that Connor will never have a chance to heal, that his life is over because of the man who'd wanted to control me. It's a tragedy really, because Connor's entire existence ended up being so much pain. He'd never truly had a chance to live.

It makes me feel a little ridiculous trying on the clothing in light of those thoughts swirling around my mind, but I'm happy to find that some of the outfits I bought on that late-night shopping spree are kind of cute and flattering.

I decide to wear a pair of dark denim jeans with a deep V-neck blouse. It's black and silky, and I put a gold chain necklace around my neck, styling my hair, doing my best to replicate what Jenna had done a few days ago. I added light makeup and then packed a bag to take to Holt's house.

I don't anticipate anything happening between him and me, but the idea of spending that much time with him does send a bit of a thrill through me. His company is not just fun, but it's soothing too. His presence is comforting and makes me wonder how my presence makes him feel.

Later, I get in my car. It's strange not enabling the security system, but it's completely broken. It's all been destroyed. So instead of setting alarms, I simply used a key and locked my house. And the crazy part is, I don't actually have a reason to keep my house secure like I used to anymore.

Flint is dead. He's gone. Fountain of Faith is dismantled, all of it broken down in a day. I still haven't processed what that means for me, to no longer live my life thinking someone is after me.

Before I pull away from my small house in the woods, I pull up my new favorite podcast. Instead of something on psychology or trauma, I opt for something funny. One of my students recommended it a few weeks ago, saying the comedians were hilarious. Three guys host a show where they basically just talk shit and laugh, tell jokes, and I realize I need a little bit more of that in my life. For so long, I've been just focused on keeping my head above water. Anything to avoid drowning.

Now, I want to swim.

When I get to Holt's place, his apartment smells divine.

"Wow," I say as he hands me a glass of white wine. "I am impressed."

"Why? Because I'm not a messy bachelor?"

"No, because you actually did cook this meal. It smells amazing."

"I haven't done the fish yet or the asparagus, so it'll be like ten more minutes."

"I'm not in any rush to eat."

I set my things down on the couch and watch Holt as he cooks. I slide onto a bar stool at his counter.

"So," I say, "How are you doing?"

"I'm fine," he says, then turns to look at me over his shoulder. "But I didn't kill a guy yesterday."

"Wow," I say, snorting. "That's a little callous."

"Is it?" He asks, now more serious.

"Sorry, no, I'm just being silly. It's just a little strange, you know? He was my ... "

"I know," Holt says. "Your husband?"

"I was going to say my arch enemy."

"Well, I'm glad he is gone then."

"Me too."

"Are you glad you're the one who pulled the trigger?"

I set my wine glass down, running my fingers over the stem.

"Yes," I tell him, honestly. "I am. I mean, he would've killed me if I hadn't done it first. And the truth is, I think it was time for him to go."

Holt's eyes lock on mine.

"You're brave, Willow Grace."

"Stop it," I say.

"You are. You're the bravest woman I know."

"You sure? Not Lucinda? Or Victoria? Or ..."

"Don't," Holt says, now turning to face me. "You know I'm not interested in those women."

"I don't know. There's always some girl calling you."

"Don't do that," he begs.

"I'm sorry," I relent. "I was just teasing."

"I know you are, but I mean it, Willow. Those women aren't for me."

I clear my throat and take a sip of wine, wanting to change the subject as Holt plates our food. He carries it to the dining room table. I follow him, carrying his wine glass for him.

"I got a call today about a new assignment," he tells me.

"Already?"

"Yeah, there's always something new."

"Okay. And?"

"Well, my recent cases caught the attention of the head of the BAU."

We set the food and drinks down on the table and I ask, "Sorry, what's that?"

"Behavioral Analysis Unit. The mind hunters, profilers kind of like... well do you know that show Criminal Minds?"

I nod. "That's pretty cool, I think. I mean, I'm happy if you're happy." I pick up my fork and prepare to dig in. The aroma makes me salivate.

"I am. It's just, this new assignment would take me away from the area. I'd be traveling for new cases and it could take me all over the country."

I pause, my fork in the air. I haven't even taken a bite of the food.

"I'm happy for you," I murmur.

"Are you?" Holt asks, eyes boring into me, as if trying to tell me something. Ask me something.

"Why wouldn't I be? I mean, I'm happy if you're happy."

"You wouldn't miss me?"

"I didn't say that. I just ..." I shrug.

"I'm only teasing," Holt says. "I mean, I did get offered the position, but I'll only agree to take it under one condition."

"And what condition is that?" I ask him.

"That you come with me."

I set my fork down now. "Like travel with you, as your like, I don't know, lover?"

"No," Holt says. "I mean, yes, that." My stomach does a weird flip and my cheeks begin to heat. He continues talking. "I more meant, as my partner. You could be hired as a full-time consultant and serve as my direct partner."

"You want that?"

"I'd love that," he tells me plainly.

I take a big gulp of wine, shocked.

"So you would be my direct supervisor?" I smile.

"I'd rather us be equals."

I nod and contemplate for a moment. Finally I say, "Paxton?"

"Yes, Willow?"

"I'll accept the position under one condition."

"You have conditions too, huh?"

I grin. "I mean, I'm not going to work side-by-side with you if I don't even know how well you kiss." I wear an innocent expression, blinking my eyes rapidly, and take another sip of wine.

Holt laughs. "You're trouble, Willow Grace."

But he gets out of his chair and walks around the table, taking my hand and pulling me up.

"We can solve that real quick," he says. He leans down, cupping my cheeks with his hand. I close my eyes and lift my chin as his mouth meets mine. His lips are soft and insistent. Good. Great. The kiss is better than I imagined. His lips part and mine do too. For this moment, we're lost in one another.

When he pulls away and looks at me, his eyes sparkle.

"Is that a yes?" he asks.

"It's a yes. We're going to find out how we'll do as partners," I laugh. "If the kiss is any indication, I think it's going to work out great."

The story continues in *Time for Grace....*

In the claustrophobic heart of darkness, the eerie tick-tock from unseen shadows is the lone harbinger of a terrifying threat. Paralyzed by fear and an assailant's potent drug, he is robbed of defenses, except for the chilling symphony of sounds that narrate his impending doom. The last grain of sand plummets down an hourglass just as the metronomic ticking halts, leaving him in the grip of a consuming silence.

Enter Willow Grace: a psychologist steeped in cult practices, taking a pause from her university role to join the FBI at the request of Agent Paxton Holt. Their shared attraction is palpable but unexplored, a silent current beneath a sea of professional respect. Together, they're tasked to outsmart the country's most elusive criminals, chasing shadows through the murkiest depths of the human psyche.

An unsettling murder breathes life into a long-stilled investigation. Is it the return of a serial murderer known as the Hourglass Killer, or the rise of an ominous imitator? Willow and Holt find themselves on a treacherous journey into the mind of a psychopath, where trust is as fragile as a strand of spider's silk.

Each tick of the clock dials up the suspense, sand grains slipping away in a race against an enemy who toys with the delicate balance between life and death.

Can they outwit a killer who holds the shears of fate?

Pre-Order your copy of Time for Grace today!

https://www.amazon.com/gp/product/B0CB4RDJQJ

Did you enjoy *Hunt for Grace*? Leave a review and tell us what you think!

https://www.amazon.com/gp/product/B0C953Z5TL

Want to stay up to date on all things *Willow Grace*? Subscribe to the Without Warrant newsletter to receive updates on Willow Grace releases and receive 3 free Without Warrant books!

https://liquidmind.media/without-warrant-cold-newsletter-signup-1/

WILLOW GRACE SERIES

Willow Grace FBI Thrillers

Shadow of Grace

Condition of Grace

Hunt for Grace

Time for Grace

Piece of Grace (coming soon)

ALSO BY WITHOUT WARRANT

More Thriller Series from Without Warrant Authors

Dana Gray Mysteries by C.J. Cross

Girl Left Behind

Girl on the Hill

Girl in the Grave

The Kenzie Gilmore Series by Biba Pearce

Afterburn

Dead Heat

Heatwave

Burnout

Deep Heat

Fever Pitch

Storm Surge (Coming Soon)

Willow Grace FBI Thrillers

Shadow of Grace

Condition of Grace

Hunt for Grace (Coming Soon)

**Gia Santella Crime Thriller Series
by Kristi Belcamino**

Vendetta

Vigilante

Vengeance

Black Widow

Day of the Dead

Border Line

Night Fall

Stone Cold

Cold as Death

Cold Blooded

Dark Shadows

Dark Vengeance

Dark Justice

Deadly Justice

Deadly Lies

Vigilante Crime Series by Kristi Belcamino

Blood & Roses

Blood & Fire

Blood & Bone

Blood & Tears

Queen of Spades Thrillers by Kristi Belcamino

Queen of Spades

The One-Eyed Jack

The Suicide King

The Ace of Clubs

The Joker

The Wild Card

High Stakes

Poker Face

Made in United States
Troutdale, OR
04/20/2024

19320857R00110